FROST (A PARANORMAL ROMANCE)

GIOVANNA REAVES

FIND ME ON SOCIAL MEDIA

I love hearing from you, email me: gotromance@giareaves.com Sign up for my newsletter to receive updates on what I have going coming next.

Check out my website: https://giareaves.com

Join my readers group: https://www.facebook.com/groups/GiovannasSecretOneNighters/

BLURB

A chance meeting doesn't go as expected, but fate intervenes, setting the stage for an unexpected connection.

Frostland Winterbourne, nicknamed Frost, has been crushing on Zane from the first time he saw the werewolf on the cover of a fashion magazine. Even with his social standing, he never expected to meet the man in person. But what is a fae to do when Zane walks into his event-planning office one day needing his help?

Zane Moon-Blood is a single father grieving the death of his mate. He vowed never to find another mate or fall in love, but it seems he forgot about fate. When Zane walked into F.W. Events, he had no clue he was meeting a member from the famous Winterbourne family who, with a snap of their finger, could make or break a company's portfolio.

At first sight, Zane is attracted to the fae, no doubt, but does he take his second chance at love or does he walk away, risking the anger of the Winterbourne family and the fates?

CHAPTER ONE

Frostland Winterbourne, or Frost to his friends, entered F.W. Events & Services. He waved a hand, magically turning on the lights as he made his way to his office, then dropped his coat and backpack on the couch in front of his desk. Frost turned on his computer, booted it up, and then went to the company's break room to get the coffee percolating.

Although his company was small, it offered many services. Including himself, two other people worked for him. There was Bronwyn Read, his gorgeous witchy best friend who doubled as the receptionist, social media manager, and in many significant roles in the company. Then there was Havar Drake, who was their dwarf behind the scenes. Havar was their master builder, a creative designer who could turn a drab building into a work of art.

Frost simply had to explain to Havar what the client wanted, and he would take care of the rest. He sighed sadly, and it was a pity that Havar wasn't there to help him decide what flavor creamer to use in his coffee.

"French vanilla or pumpkin spice?"

"You act like it's a hard decision," Bronwyn said, popping beside him. "It's only creamer." She shrugged. "Just pick one."

"It's a tough choice because I love them both."

"Then have pumpkin spice now and vanilla later."

Frost smiled. "Good idea." He got to work making two cups for them both.

Although she seemed noncommittal to his creamer issue, Bronwyn was just as fussy about their coffee and creamer. It was why they were best friends. Not only that, neither would admit they were caffeine addicts.

When Frost started F.W. Events, he knew he couldn't have done it without his best friend by his side. Frost and Bronwyn were neighbors and grew up together in Wynter Spell, a well-hidden magical town in the North Pole.

"Did you hear the news about your cousin, Bluebell?" Bronwyn asked, ready to give the latest tea on outer-world gossip.

"Don't tell me he got into trouble again." Bluebell Boroson was an elf and known to only a select few to be the great-grandson of Nick Boroson, the man known to the world as Santa Claus. Frost had been happy to hear that his cousin Bluebell was an elf and got his dream job as a wish agent for Santa's Workshop. Bluebell and many elves and fae lived in the magical town of Wynter Spell. Frost's mother, Bell Sterling, was one of the youngest sisters of Nick Boroson and a born demi-fae. She was the daughter of the god Odin, who now went by the last name Boroson and lived in the magical town of Vale Valley with his wife, Rosemary Vale, who was a distant relative to Bronwyn.

Vale Valley and Wynter Spell weren't the only magical towns. There were quite a few, like Valleywood and others hiding in certain pockets of the world that only a select few knew they existed. After the great war between supernaturals, most sects created their own realms, separating themselves from the human world. The Nyxian sect came to mind. Also, there was a place that Frost visited often that not even other supernaturals knew about. The realm of the in-between where the most powerful gods, angel demons, and other beings lived—when they were not causing trouble on the Earth realm.

The world was fascinating to him, and in his young fae age, he wanted to know more. It was why his business, F.W. Planning, sat in between the realms, catering to both humans' and supernaturals' needs. His office was like a magical portal and called to those who needed his service no matter their state, country, or continent.

"He did," Bronwyn said, sipping her coffee.

"Well, what did he do?" Frost asked, eager to know what trouble his old friend had gotten into.

"I don't know. I thought you'd know since you're related to him."

"How would I? I haven't spoken to Bluebell for about a year. Besides, you know how secretive wish elves are."

"Yeah." She sadly sighed. "Why didn't you want to work for Santa's Workshop? Do you know how much fun we could have had? Plus the gossip." Her eyes and face lit up as she spoke.

Santa's Workshop wasn't just a place that made toys his uncle delivered on Christmas Eve night. The wishes granted throughout the year lent to the magic that kept Wynter Spell hidden and safe and aided in other jobs at Santa's Workshop.

"Nah," Frost said. "I love my extended family, and although working alongside my uncle Nick might be cool, I prefer being the boss. Besides, if you look at our work, we fulfill wishes just like Santa's helpers. And as residents of Wynter Spell, what we do also spreads to the town. Even when we don't use magic, our clients are always happy with our service."

"True. You downplay it so much I sometimes forget that's how you set things up. You really are a powerful fae, Frost." Bronwyn smiled. "Maybe we should take an impromptu trip to Wynter Spell instead of waiting until Christmas Eve. By then, everyone would be too busy giving your uncle some strength."

Every Christmas Eve, former and current residents gathered in Wynter Spell and infused Nick with their magic to help him deliver presents to the entire world in one night. Even gods needed help once in a while.

"You just want to go to find out what Bluebell got in trouble for," Frost said, and she gave him the duh expression.

Frost chuckled and shook his head. His friend was a real gossiper, but he couldn't deny she had a good point. He was just as curious as she was and didn't know if he could wait until Christmas Eve.

Frost tilted his head. "How did you find out?"

"I bumped into our old friend, Flake, who works with your cousin and couldn't help yapping about your cousin fucking up but wouldn't tell me what he did. Now he's on desk duty for gods knows how long."

Frost knew how hard Bluebell had trained to become a wish agent, only to have Flake laugh at his expense. Flake was forever getting under both his and Bluebell's skin when they were growing up. It didn't help that Bluebell and Frost constantly played tricks on Flake as payback for being annoying.

"Maybe we should pay Bluebell a visit?" Frost said,

knowing how upset Bluebell might've been at himself for fucking up on the job he loved more than anything else. It didn't help that Bluebell's department head was Callum Boroson, his father.

Frost shivered at the thought of working for any of his family members. He hated being micromanaged. Unlike his family, Frost had no qualms about using some magic in the presence of humans who would marvel that he was a great magician. Frost was an ice elemental fae and, according to his parents, unique. While most of his kin did not like meddling in human lives, Frost found them interesting. He seemed to learn something new from his human clients each time he worked with them. Years ago, when he started F.W. Events, it was on a dare from his older brother that he couldn't last a year without relying on his trust fund.

Before he became a respectable business owner, Frost loved to party and played pranks on his friends and family, which didn't draw laughter but irritation and anger. He didn't care about being responsible or contributing to his family's wealth. He enjoyed life the way he thought he should live. His older brother, Nyx, had grown tired of Frost's childish ways and dared him to hold down a job for one year; then he wouldn't deem Frost irresponsible. But if he lost his job, Frost would have to work in the family company. Though his brother thought otherwise, Frost was confident he'd win the bet. However, he didn't know exactly how he would win because he didn't enjoy working for others.

He'd thought long and hard about what he was good at, and the only thing that came to him was that he loved to party, and that included planning them. For any events he'd had, Frost would be the one to organize them with flair and extravagance. Initially, Frost figured he'd work for one year, do a few jobs, and get Nyx off his back. What he didn't count on was that in a matter of weeks after opening, he would be so busy and in need of help that he ended up hiring his friend Bronwyn.

Although he had won the bet, his brother did not lose out either. Frost loved his job and worked with various people, including humans who didn't know about magic and immortals who weren't good at event planning. Since business had been going so great, Frost had been thinking of hiring more people and making Bronwyn a true partner.

"So, what's on our schedule for today?" he asked, setting Bronwyn's coffee in front of her since she was already sitting at her desk.

It was the day after Thanksgiving weekend, and it was also the time when he got busy planning winter weddings and office Christmas and New Year parties.

"The invitation for Lisa Staetum and Mark Anderson's wedding came in after you left last Friday, so they'll need to be dropped off sometime today. The venue model is done, so they can work on the seating chart once they receive RSVPs."

Lisa and Mark had shown up in his office three weeks ago, begging him to plan their elaborate wedding for the night before Christmas Eve. Frost would have turned them down since it was short notice, but he couldn't walk away from the challenge that came with the job.

"Where is the model?"

"In the workroom," Bronwyn answered.

Bronwyn stood from her desk and went into the work-room, where they kept model designs and various supplies. For every job they took on, no matter how small the project was, Frost ensured a visual model was done so their clients could envision their special day. Drinking the last of his coffee, Frost followed Bronwyn and inspected the Anderson model. He had to admit he loved the changes they'd suggested. It was a winter replica of the Trevi Fountain, with floating lanterns and candles surrounding the room. Although they would be inside, the venue was surrounded in nothing but glass.

Waving a hand, Frost added the snow the bride hoped would fall, adding more romance to the event. But if it didn't, Frost had a way of making things happen. He turned marble figures into moving ice sculptures that changed positions every ten minutes. They might even dance around the room if he so chose. It took a little magic to make the venue look precisely how Lisa and Mark wanted, and since they were human, they'd never know that little information.

"Havar did a good job on this one," Frost acknowledged.

"He did," Bronwyn said, nodding. "To think he almost didn't get it done."

"What?" Frost said in shock. "What was the delay?"

Bronwyn sighed. "He's still upset you won't go out with him."

Frost rolled his eyes. "How often do I need to tell him I don't date people I work with?"

Havar was a handsome, sweet, sexy redhead elf with chocolate-brown eyes that Frost adored. However, he felt nothing other than friendship for the man. Frost wanted to fall in love and feel the connection he'd only heard of from his family members when they found their mate. Sadness crept up in his heart, and he quickly pushed it down. He didn't want to think about how lonely he was, even with the hordes of friends and lovers he had at his beck and call.

"I'll take the model and invitations to Lisa and Mark at two today," he told Bronwyn.

"You can't," she said hurriedly. "You have a new client coming today."

"Oh, then I'll drop it off after the meeting." Bronwyn nodded. "Also, order a light lunch for me. I'll be in my office if you need me."

"What do you want?"

"Hmm...let's go with a salad and no onions. Don't want to meet a new client with bad breath."

Bronwyn chuckled. "Sounds good."

LATER THAT DAY, Frost was engrossed in completing his paperwork. He was startled out of his thoughts when Bronwyn spoke as she entered his office.

"Your two o'clock appointment is here."

"Okay, thanks for telling me." He ran his fingers through his moderately long snow-white hair. "Give me a few minutes, then show them in." He started cleaning up his desk when he noticed she was still there. "Is there something else?"

"Aren't you going to ask me who it is?"

Frost furrowed his brows. "Didn't you already tell me who it is?"

"Nope."

"Then out with it. Who am I meeting with?" Frost wasn't in the mood to play around. He had been in a foul mood since he'd thought about how lonely he was. Plus, he had a lot of things to do before meeting with Lisa and Mark that evening.

Bronwyn leaned closer to him, smirking as if she had a secret she couldn't wait to tell him. "Zane Blood-Moon."

Frost's eyes widened. "Za...Zane Blood-Moon. You

mean the tall, dark, and devilishly handsome man is in my office right now? Tell me you're fucking with me."

"I would never fuck with you on something like this," Bronwyn said, smiling. "Boss, your crush is waiting to speak with you. I'd try to get with him if I weren't already mated. He's so much better-looking in person."

"Shit." Frost stood, flustered and seeming unsure of himself. "I can't meet him."

"What? Why?"

Frost looked at her as if she had lost all of her marbles. No one ever expected to meet their crush, especially one like Zane Blood-Moon, who was an alpha wolf. The man had started his career as a model, making Frost and many others lust after him. Zane had a milk-chocolate brown complexion, dark curly shoulder-length hair that he shaved on the sides and back, hazel eyes, chiseled hard muscles, and a killer smile. Frost wanted to say he knew everything about the sexiest alpha since first seeing him on a magazine cover, but Zane had disappeared and showed up six years later as the CEO of Blood-Moon Technologies, with offices worldwide.

"I don't think I'd be able to speak to him."

"You're talking nonsense."

"I'm being for real." He looked down at his wrinkled shirt, which had a stain on it. He really couldn't meet the man looking like a slob. "I need a fresh shirt." Waving a hand, he sent his magic to the small apartment he'd built connected to his office, getting an extra shirt and changing into it while he spoke to Bronwyn.

"Why didn't you tell me he was the person I was meeting with?"

"I didn't know," Bronwyn said. "It was supposed to be Mrs. Marvins."

"Fuck, so what does he want?"

"For you to plan a party, duh," she said, rolling her eyes.

"I know that, smartass. I need to know what kind of party, and please don't say wedding because it will break my damn heart."

"It's not a wedding."

Frost sighed dramatically.

"Good gods, I've never seen you like this."

"What are you talking about? I'm not acting any differently than I would for another client."

"Keep telling yourself that. Anyway, he wants us to plan his company's New Year's Eve party."

"New Years! Is he crazy?" They had enough time to plan something simple, but if he wanted a more elaborate gathering, it would be a challenge. "Does he already have a venue?"

"Nope."

"Fuck, what is he thinking?"

"You can ask him that when you meet him." She walked to the door. "I have him in the conference room."

Pulling on his suit jacket, a few thoughts came to him. "Did you..."

"He prefers tea to coffee and cupcakes to cookies," Bronwyn said, as if knowing what he was thinking. "Anything else?"

"No. Just let him know I'll be out in a few minutes. Make something up like I'm on a call so he doesn't think I'm...you know."

"Yeah, yeah, I get it. Don't forget your tie."

Bronwyn left his office, and Frost took a few minutes to collect his racing heart. "Remember, Frost, he's just like any other client. So what if you have a crush on him? Put that aside and focus on your job. Besides, you might have to reject his request, anyway." Frost walked to the conference room, taking large steps like the boss he was. When he opened the doors, he didn't waste any time with foolishness and quickly introduced himself.

"Hello, Mr. Gorgeous, I'm Bloody-Moon and want to fuck you." The second he said it, Frost felt his face turn so red he was ready to run out of the room, yet if he ran, it would make him look like a bigger idiot.

CHAPTER TWO

Zane smirked, then cleared his throat, trying to hold back his chuckle at the other man's slip of the tongue.

"Mr. Frostland Winterbourne, I presume." He extended a hand, but the man hadn't pulled out of his stupor. He simply turned a shade of red, making his alabaster complexion look like a ripe tomato. Zane bit his lips, really trying to stop himself from laughing. Zane knew about the Winterbourne organization. At one point, he thought they were a part of the mafia because of their reputation and vast wealth.

Zane had always wondered if they were of the supernatural nature, and from the earthy, minty scent with a touch of pine coming off the man, he could tell Winterbourne was a fae. Zane knew little about faes, only that they were possessive and temperamental. Zane had been trying to meet with Nyx Winterbourne, the heir to the family business. Zane was looking for someone with more power than him to invest in a new game his company was developing.

Zane couldn't recall how he'd come across the company name, F.W. Events. It just so happened that one day he was in the area, saw the business name, and sent the information to his secretary to set up a meeting. But after doing his research and recognizing the Winterbourne name, Zane told his secretary that he would take over the party planning. Zane figured if he could get close to this Winterbourne, maybe he could meet the older brother.

But Zane had to admit, the pictures he'd seen of the younger Winterbourne had not done the man justice, or maybe it was just him. The fae's cobalt-blue eyes were so bright that they seemed unreal. Not to mention his striking white hair that resembled snow, giving credence to his name, Frost.

"Mr. Winterbourne."

"Huh?" They both stared at each other before the man's eyes widened. "Fuck, I'm not being professional." He bashfully looked away from Zane, whispering, but he heard him. "Who told you to be so good-looking?"

"Um..." Zane cleared his throat again, trying to hide his chuckle. He pulled his extended hand back, shoving it in his pocket and quirking a brow.

"I'm not usually this unprofessional, Mister Blood-Moon," the fae said.

"It's fine," Zane said with a smile, hoping it would ease the awkwardness.

"How about we start fresh?"

"I'm game if you are."

Winterbourne closed his eyes and took a couple of deep breaths, giving Zane time to study the man more. He was shorter than Zane, around five-foot-six by his estimation, complementing his lean physique. A few seconds later, Winterbourne opened his eyes, and Zane could see the slight change in his demeanor.

The fae extended a hand to Zane with a smile. "Hello,

Mister Blood-Moon, welcome to F.W. Events. I'm Frostland Winterbourne, but you can call me Frost."

Zane took the hand offered and froze as a warm, plea-surable feeling ran down his spine. The scent of pine and mint intensified, making him feel like shifting into his wolf and rolling around in the scent.

Why does this feel so familiar? Mate?

The second the word passed through Zane's thoughts, he instantly released the fae's hand, stepping back as if the other man's touch had singed him.

"It's nice..." He took a deep breath, trying to shake the feeling and think of something else. "It's nice to meet you."

Winterbourne stared at him for a few seconds too long, and Zane loosened his tie that suddenly felt as if it were trying to choke the living shit out of him.

"You..." He pointed at Zane. "You're..."

"I'm here to conduct business, Mister Winterbourne." He had no choice but to cut the fae off because he wasn't ready to hear what the man had to say. "I know it's short notice, but according to your glowing reviews, you are the best person for the job. Usually, I'd leave these types of things to my secretary, but I wanted to do this for the employees in my company who've been there from the beginning. The party must happen in less than six weeks." Zane knew he was babbling, but he couldn't help it. The thought of finding a new mate left him a bit unsettled. "I have a theme in mind; I wasn't the one that came up with it." He smirked, thinking of his seven-year-old daughter Hannah, the genius behind it. "I was thinking of a holiday fairy tale ball on New Year's Eve. Where everyone can let their imagination out."

"Is that all you're going to say?" the fae asked, visibly upset.

"Did I miss something, Mister Winterbourne?"

"What the fuck? Yes, you missed something." The fae's blue eyes burned into Zane. "We're..."

"Conducting business, or should I go to your competitor?" Zane couldn't let Frost finish his words. If the words were left unsaid, then the matter wouldn't be rejected.

"Is that how you feel?" Winterbourne questioned, as if knowing what Zane was thinking.

Zane looked away from the other man's gaze, unable to give him a straight answer.

"I see," Winterbourne whispered. "Then, Mister Blood-Moon, I can't help you."

Zane turned his head just in time to see the fae walking out of the conference room. Zane knew he should go after Winterbourne, but that would mean admitting he had found his second mate after losing the love of his life.

TWELVE YEARS AGO, Zane had fallen madly and deeply in love with whom he thought was the most beautiful woman in the world. Arizona Ravenson Hart, a model he had met at a fashion show, knew she was his mate the instant they saw each other. They'd been paired in some shoots, and Zane didn't waste a moment conversing and getting to know her. After the fashion show, they spent time together before they had to leave for their next modeling job.

Zane took Arizona to dinner, and they spent the entire night getting to know each other. He became enamored by her smile; her light brown eyes captivated him. He found the way Arizona twirled her fingers around her dark brown curls adorable. She had an intellect and wit that kept a smile on Zane's face. Also, she didn't look at him weirdly when he explained his reasons for becoming a model.

Zane had never met anyone like Arizona and knew he had to claim her before they separated. So that night, during their walk after dinner, he told her he was a werewolf and explained as much as he could about the supernatural world. However, Zane was the one who was floored when she told him she knew he was a werewolf. Although she was human, she came from a long line of witches. She wasn't born with any witchy powers herself, but her family never made her feel any less because of it. Not only that, she had family living all over the United States, from Cypress Prince to Valleywood.

Although he was a werewolf, Zane had never known that magical city existed, and he was certain he wasn't the only one. Zane was an orphan and grew up in Cypress Prince and knew of the Pryde pack, who, until recently, were enemies with the large vampire sect that dwelled in the city. He'd considered contacting Duncan Pryde about being a part of his sect a time or two.

However, he was a werewolf with only a tiny drop of lykosian blood. He wasn't sure how accepting the sect would be to him. Also, Zane had stayed away from the sect after hearing about some of the trouble they had been getting up to. After learning about Valleywood, Zane had thought about moving there when he and Arizona had mated, since the magic would better protect her. But Arizona suggested they stay in Cypress Prince.

He smiled, recalling her words to him that night. *"There are things in life that cannot be explained. I was born without powers, yet I met a werewolf and part Lykosian who wants to claim me. I can say that I'm pretty lucky."*

Still, with her accepting nature, Zane told her she could

walk away. He was a rogue, a wolf without a pack, and did not plan to align himself with one, so the only one who could protect her was him. He wasn't wealthy, although he had big ideas at the time to start his own technology company. Zane wasn't sure how long it would take. But she told him that none of that mattered to her. She planned on staying by his side and supporting his dream.

That night, they were mated and became inseparable, or tried to remain close to each other because of their occupation. Zane and Arizona kept their relationship a secret, only telling a couple of their trusted friends everything in Zane's world was going great. He was in love, and two years after meeting Arizona, they had saved enough for him to start his tech company, and he could quit modeling while Arizona kept working because she loved it more than he did.

As time passed, Arizona got pregnant with their daughter. He was so damn happy he almost bought out the entire baby store. He pampered his pregnant mate for her entire pregnancy. Nine months later, she delivered a healthy baby, bringing joy to them both. But that joy only lasted a few years before Arizona was killed in a car crash while on a modeling job in Italy.

Zane ran his fingers through his short, curly hair. After her death, he had lived in a world of pain and refused to think or talk about it. But as time passed, the pain lessened, but the feeling of losing Arizona never went away. Her place in his heart remained strong, and at times, he could feel her presence around him. Zane sighed as he walked over to the window, feeling like he was looking into another world. Or maybe it had been like that for him since Arizona's death.

Others had probably said it many times, but Zane stood

by his words. Finding another mate was never in his plans. After her death, Zane focused on his daughter and building his business. He couldn't picture himself with anyone other than the mother of his child. He and Arizona had many years together, and they'd wanted so much more.

Zane's parents had passed away before he started modeling, but it didn't hurt as much as when Arizona died. He avoided love to not feel that pain again. Zane could honestly say if it weren't for Hannah, he would have sunk into a world of despair. His sweet girl looked more like her mother, but had none of her calm temperament. Hannah was more like him and was bravely outspoken at her young age.

He couldn't imagine how she would react if he told her he had found his mate. Would she feel betrayed by Zane? Or think that he was replacing her mother with someone new? Hannah never asked or talked about having another parent, even with her brazenness. He had to consider her feelings.

"Fuck, what do I do?" Sighing, he closed his eyes, hoping to get some answers, but nothing came to mind.

"Oh, I'm sorry. I thought the room was empty."

Zane opened his eyes and turned to the voice, seeing that it was the witch who worked for Winterbourne. Zane had completely forgotten her name in the short time since they'd met.

"I'm glad you're still here, Mister Blood-Moon. I needed to speak with you about the details of your event. Since it's short notice, a lot of work needs to be done, so if you have time, we can go over them right now."

Zane's brows furrowed as he stood straight, looking at the witch. "I don't understand. I thought your boss turned me down."

"I don't know what was discussed between you two, but our company will handle your company party."

"No," Zane said, cutting her off.

"Excuse me?" she countered, abrasive, which Zane ignored.

"The person I'll work with is your boss." Zane didn't know what in the fuck he was saying or doing, but for some reason, he would only be satisfied if Winterbourne worked on his project.

"Are you always this rude?" the witch asked.

"Not normally," Zane said. "But I think you and possibly your boss misunderstood something. Where is Winterbourne?"

"Frost left. He had another appointment."

"When will he be back?"

"I don't know." She crossed her arms over her chest, glaring at Zane as if to say she knew but would not tell him shit.

She was an excellent guard dog, was all Zane could think. He was certain that the witch had no clue what had really happened between him and Winterbourne, but she would protect him. However, her actions angered Zane. It wasn't her job to protect Winterbourne. That was the duty of the alpha mate. But of course, Zane had to rein in his emotions and thoughts since he had yet to utter the sentence: *Winterbourne is my mate.*

"Tell your boss I'll be in to see him tomorrow," Zane said, walking to the door.

"You need an appointment to meet with Frost," the witch told him.

Zane smirked. "I don't need an appointment to see my —" He paused for a second before selecting his choice of words. "Trust me, he'll want to see me. Because no matter what, he can't hide from me."

Zane walked out of F.W. Events with confused emotions and highly annoyed. Yet, he was unsure who he was irritated with, himself or Winterbourne.

"Fuck, what the hell was I thinking?"

CHAPTER THREE

"What happened between you and Blood-Moon?" Bronwyn asked, bursting into his office. "For a good-looking man, he really has a nasty attitude."

"Nothing," Frost said as he continued to work, not turning in Bronwyn's direction.

After storming out of the conference room, Frost wasn't sure why he did it, but he took on the job. However, Bronwyn would handle everything. Frost was so hurt that he felt numb. He didn't think after finding his mate that he'd be rejected, even if Zane hadn't said the words out loud. His attitude implied it. Frost rubbed his chest, hoping to feel the sense of loss, wanting to curse the fates for sending a man his way who did not want him.

"I need you to put out some job offers, to fill some positions," he told her.

"What? Why?"

Frost heard her question and the worry that went with her tone, and should soothe her, but his mind was still on the conversation that happened in the conference room.

"Frost, why are you so silent?" Bronwyn spoke, bringing him back to his senses. "Are you firing me?"

His brows furrowed as he finally looked at her. "Why would you ask such a ridiculous question?"

"Then why do you want to hire more people?"

"Bronwyn, do you think you can plan an event in six weeks *and* manage the office? Even with using magic, I won't put that pressure on you. It's time we hire more people to fill positions in the office. We need a creative director, more event planners, and all the other openings we have. The work needs to be divided since you and Havar will be made partners."

"Wait...wait, what's with this partner business? Frost, what brought this on?"

"It's something that I've been thinking about for awhile. Even though this started out to win a bet between me and my brother, things turned out far better than I expected. You and Havar have been with me since the beginning; it's only right that you both get a piece of the pie."

"Can I think about it?" she asked after a few seconds of silence.

"Of course," Frost said. "Take all the time you need. But whether you accept the partnership or not, you will be getting your own office."

"Fine, I know I'm not going to talk you out of it, so do as you please."

"Don't I always."

Frost went back to work but stopped when he felt Bronwyn's looming presence over him. "What's the matter?"

"Are you going to answer my question? What happened in the conference room?"

"I told you, nothing happened."

"We've been friends since childhood, you think I can't

tell when you're lying to me or trying to avoid situations? Talk to me," Bronwyn prodded. "You're making me worry."

"It's nothing." He smiled. "I'm just having an off moment. Maybe it's meeting my crush and all that."

"You don't look like you're happy about it. Usually, when something good goes your way, you float around here, and your feet hardly touch the ground."

Frost closed his eyes. "Bronwyn, please, let's just get back to work."

"Fine, but I'm not the one he wants working on his event," Bronwyn told him. "He was quite insistent that it should be you."

Frost snapped open his eyes, peering at Bronwyn. "What the hell do you mean by that?" She went to respond, but Frost decided he did not want to hear it. "You know what? Forget it. Just handle the job and make sure he and I never interact."

"That's impossible, I'll need your approval on some things."

"See, if you were to agree to a partnership, you wouldn't." Frost smiled when she rolled her eyes. "Just do as I told you and remember to send out the job postings."

Knowing that Bronwyn would want to talk more about the Zane thing when he didn't want to, Frost stood and grabbed his suit jacket off the floor. He'd flung it in anger after entering his office and now hurriedly shrugged it on. "I'll take the model to Lisa and Mark. You don't have to worry about it."

Bronwyn grabbed his hand when he walked by her and reached for the door. "Frost, talk to me. I know something is bothering you."

Frost patted her hand. "Not right now."

They stared at each other, and Bronwyn nodded in

understanding. Taking her hand away, Frost smiled reassuringly before leaving his office. Frost couldn't help but think of the irony as he gathered everything he needed. Hours ago, he was happily planning someone else's forever. Now, he just felt empty since his mate had rejected him.

What a way to start the holiday! Fuck, I need to stay busy. The more time I think about Zane Blood-Moon, the more depressed I'll get.

HOURS LATER, Frost barged into his older brother's office, ignoring that Nyx was having a meeting, and went straight for the liquor. He grabbed a bottle of Absinthe, poured a glass, and took a shot of the sweet liquor that left a smooth aftertaste as it went down, sending warmth through him.

It wasn't enough to make him forget his hurt, and Frost quickly poured another, but before he could drink it, the glass was snatched from him.

"Hey," he yelled, reaching for his glass but was unsuccessful. He disliked being shorter than Nyx at that moment. "Give that back."

"Not until you tell me what's going on with you."

Frost went to drink from the bottle since his brother was a right dick, but that was taken away from him, too.

"Nothing is bothering me," he lied.

"I didn't send my people away for no reason so go try telling that to some idiot who didn't grow up with you. Besides, you only drink this shit when you're pissed off about something. Now talk to me," Nyx ordered.

Frost stared at his brother, who had been his protector in every way. Growing up, Nyx would kick anyone's ass who tried to talk shit or raise a hand against Frost. Also, his older brother spoiled him to pieces and would do anything to make Frost happy. They may be elves related to Nicholas Boroson, known as Santa Claus, and often liked to spread Christmas cheer, but they weren't always nice to the ones who hurt them.

"I want you to kick his ass! Better yet, buy his company and make him go broke," Frost raged. "Ruin his life, Nyx. Do it for me."

Nyx's brows knitted in a tight crease at Frost's outburst. "Whose life am I taking away now? Who hurt you?"

"My mate..." He stepped away from Nyx, needing air since his temper was rising as he thought about Zane Blood-Moon's rejection. "Well, we're not mated yet, but I felt our connection and know he felt it too. But he wants to act like nothing happened, and he hurt me, so go kick his ass!"

"Have I spoiled you so much that you see me as some servant you can order around easily?" Nyx huffed, walking over to him.

"But he..." Frost hiccuped as the liquor he drank took effect. Truthfully, he had a low alcohol tolerance but didn't care how drunk he got. He just wanted to forget the pain in his heart. "He doesn't want me, Nyx."

Frost grabbed the bottle from Nyx's hand and took a large swig before it was taken away from him. Frost cleaned off his mouth with the back of his hand. "He couldn't even look at me when he rejected me."

"Who rejected you?" Nyx growled.

"My mate," Frost slurred. "Aren't you listening to me?"

"Who is he, Frostland? I need the name of the asshole who rejected my baby brother."

"Blood..." Frost hiccuped. "Blood-Moon ... Zane Blood-Moon."

Nyx stepped away from Frost and moved over to his desk. "Jackson," he said softly after pressing the intercom.

"Yes, sir."

"Get me every damn thing you can find on Zane Blood-Moon. Don't leave out a single information."

"Yes, sir."

Nyx walked back over to Frost and pulled him into his embrace. "Come on, let's sit down, and you can tell me what happened."

"He rejected me...his mate...what more is there to say?"

"I know," Nyx said. "But humor your big brother."

Frost went to get another bottle of liquor to help him get through his short tale, but Nyx stopped him and led him over to the sofa in his office.

"Why won't you let me drink my troubles away!"

"You've had plenty," Nyx snapped.

"One drink is not enough," Frost complained. "I need to drown my sorrows."

"You know you're a lightweight. I'm kind of surprised you're not already passed out on your ass," Nyx grumbled.

"It's not me you need to be concerned with. It's the fucker who doesn't want me."

"Sit down and explain things to me."

Frost flopped down on the couch like a petulant child. "I don't want to talk about it. I want you to kick Blood-Moon's ass." Frost couldn't understand why his brother was stalling.

He glanced at Nyx, who had a muscular build for an elf and was good at fighting since he boxed every day. He couldn't recall his brother being afraid to square off against anyone.

Wait, could that be it? Is he afraid of Zane Blood-Moon?

Frost thought about it for a second. *Nah, it's never in Nyx's nature to back down from anyone or anything.*

"I will do as you ask if you simply tell me what happened today."

Frost stared at his brother. "Promise?"

"Have I ever broken a vow to you?"

"Nothing that's important to me," Frost said, shaking his head.

"Go on."

Frost took a deep breath and told Nyx everything, from when he saw Zane Blood-Moon on a magazine cover to when they shook hands in the conference room.

"Maybe he's not your mate," Nyx said, shocking Frost.

"How could he not be? I felt..." He paused, unable to find the right words to describe the warmth and desire he'd experienced just touching the man for a split second. "I can't explain it, but he's my mate."

"Or it could be you were just excited about meeting your crush and got offended that he didn't find you as irresistible as all the other men whose asses I've had to kick over the years for trying to get in your bed."

Frost rolled his eyes. "I'm not a virgin, Nyx, and there haven't been that many."

"Whatever," Nyx grumbled. "I'm a little offended you didn't tell me about your infatuation with this Blood-Moon guy."

"Bro, I don't tell you everything I feel or think. Some things need to remain a secret. I'm sure you don't tell me everything."

Nyx chuckled, hugging Frost tighter. "You're right."

"Let's do this. I'll wait for the information on Blood-Moon to come in, and when I get it, I'll let you know the important bits."

Frost considered his brother's words and felt strange in his gut.

"Do you know something about Blood-Moon that you're not telling me?"

Nyx flicked him on the nose lightly. "Stop thinking crazy. I know only about his business dealings. His personal life is a mystery."

"Okay, but what do I do in the meantime?"

"Live your life as normal. I'm sure we'll find out something soon. We have some important connections, after all." Nyx smiled.

Frost knew who his brother was referring to, but would Bluebell help them was the question?

Nyx kissed him on the side of the head, and Frost had to admit he felt sleepy suddenly. So he closed his eyes and snuggled against his big brother, letting him protect him while he slept.

THE FOLLOWING MORNING, an exhausted Zane was finishing up Hannah's scrambled eggs while the business news played in the background. He had spent most of the night thinking about a certain fae. He paused mid scramble when BM Technologies was mentioned. It was not unusual, however what made his ear perk up was the report that his stocks had taken a drastic slump before the stock market had even opened.

"What the ever loving fuck?" Zane growled. He turned off the burner and grabbed his cellphone and called his assistant. "Make sure everyone is in my office by the time I get there," he ordered then hung up, not waiting for a confirmation.

Setting his phone down, he looked at the news as anger burned in the pit of his stomach. Business was a tricky thing; one minute you could be up and another you could lose everything you'd worked for. But there was always a reason for the slump. When the markets had closed yesterday, BM Tech was sitting high, so Zane was uncertain what had happened, and it seemed even the report was a little confused as well.

"Someone has to be fucking with me." A quick thought came to him that it could be Winterbourne, but he didn't think the fae would be so petty or have that much power to fuck with his company's stock just because he wouldn't discuss the whole mating thing.

Maybe he thinks you rejected him, a voice said in the back of his mind. Zane hadn't thought of that possibility. *Fuck, I'm going to have to clear things up.*

"Daddy, is breakfast ready?" came a sweet voice behind him.

Zane pasted a smile on his face, pushing down his anger and turning to greet his little girl. Hannah was dressed in her school uniform, and all that was left for him was to fix her hair. After Arizona's death, he became a single father and had to learn how to do Hannah's mop of thick curls she got from her mom.

"How about we do your hair first and then you can eat?"

"Okay," she agreed.

They headed back up to her room, and Zane quickly did a ponytail before they headed back to the kitchen. While she ate, Zane fixed her lunch and took the time to talk with her and check to make sure Hannah had packed her homework.

"I won't be able to take you to school today," Zane told her.

"Why?" she whined.

"I have to take care of something at the office. I'll ask Megan to take you today."

"Okay, I like Megan." She looked up from her plate. "Daddy, do you like Megan?"

Zane's brows furrowed. "What's with that question?"

Hannah shrugged or tiny shoulders. "Nothing, just curious."

"Oh. Well, hurry up and eat."

"So?" she prodded.

"So what?" Zane asked, sending a text to Megan who lived next door and was a student teacher currently at Hannah's school.

"Do you like Megan?"

"Yes, she's a very nice lady," Zane answered and smiled when Megan agreed to take Hannah to school. "Megan has agreed to take you to school and home. Be on your best behavior."

"I will, Daddy." Hannah smiled.

"Good." He leaned down and kissed her forehead. "How about we make a date this weekend to put up the Christmas decorations?"

"I can't," Hannah said, surprising Zane.

"And why not?"

"I have plans."

"You're only seven. What kind of plans?"

"There's a new game coming out that I want to play."

"Wow, I got sidelined for a game."

"Don't be jealous, Daddy," she said, giving him a pitying look. "Maybe you should hang out with your friends. Oh, I know, maybe you should take Megan to the movies or something."

Zane looked at his daughter suspiciously. What was

with her fascination with Megan all of a sudden? "I don't think that's a good idea."

"Why not?"

"Enough with the questions. I'm going up to get dressed." Zane sighed when she listened that time, heading up the stairs as the troubles of his company came back to him.

CHAPTER FOUR

Zane sat in his car, staring at the office of F.W. Events. He should've been at the office dealing with the shitstorm that just landed in his lap. The only thing he'd been able to find out was that someone had anonymously reported that his company stocks were worthless. And now he was scrambling to assure his investors that everything was fine. He had been able to calm the roaring seas for now, but he had to find ways to fix the problem.

Yet, with everything happening, Zane showed up at F.W. He wasn't a narcissist by any means, but there was a nagging thought in the far back of his mind that Winterbourne might have had something to do with his company troubles. Zane didn't have evidence, so he couldn't confront the fae on it. But the idea that the man was so upset with him for not discussing the whole mate issue didn't make him as angry as it should have.

If it's his doing, then what a petty, temperamental man. Undeniably adorable but temperamental.

Zane looked in the rearview mirror, noticing the bags under his eyes. He had spent most of the night tossing and turning because he couldn't get the fae's disappointed expression out of his mind after Zane had ignored their connection. It wasn't his intention, but meeting his mate wasn't something he was expecting. Zane figured it would be best to explain things to Winterbourne, and maybe the fae would forgive him and be able to move on and find a new mate. Zane grimaced and rubbed his aching stomach at the thought of Winterbourne being someone else's.

"Fuck, how have things advanced so quickly, and all we did was shake hands?" He groaned, pressing his head on the seat headrest.

Zane sat back and stared at the building, not for the first time. A strange thought came to his mind, that there was something odd about the place. It was as if the building did not belong there and was shrouded in the same magic surrounding Valleywood.

Zane noticed that the stores and offices near Winterbourne's place were more extensive and more impressive, while the event-planning business was smaller and less noticeable. However, Zane knew the place was huge on the inside. If someone wasn't paying attention or didn't require their services, they could walk by the building without noticing it. When he walked into the building, he recalled a warm and inviting feeling and had thought nothing of it.

Illusion magic.

A while back Zane had read a little about illusion magic. It was the arts that tricked the mind into imagining unreal things.

"Could that be the reason? Maybe the building's magic orchestrated the whole mate thing."

He quickly shook his head, dispelling the thought. Just as the world evolved, so did magic. It was drawn to curious minds. However, Zane did not believe the fae would use it to trick someone into thinking they were mates. He did not seem like that kind of person. Zane wasn't sure how he knew that, but the feeling settled in the depths of his gut.

"No sense delaying things."

Zane got out of the car and walked inside, expecting to see the receptionist sitting at her desk. But he paused midstep, seeing a wonder before his eyes. The Thanksgiving decorations from the day before had been replaced with the most majestic winter wonderland. Instead of a Christmas tree, there was a giant snow globe in the reception area, but it did not obstruct anyone's view. But what caught his eye were the images playing like a movie, with people going about their day. Zane felt it was all real and nothing fabricated. However, his brows rose when the people turned and waved at him as if they knew he was watching them. Zane wasn't sure what kind of magic Winterbourne used to make it seem real, but he liked it.

There were many other things, like a slide made of snow that shouldn't have fit in the room but, oddly, worked very well. Next to the slide were piles of snow that would take different shapes, from a snowman to snow angels. Wondering if the snow was real or confetti, Zane walked over, picked some up, and was surprised that it was real snow that had a hint of fresh mint.

"Wow, this is unbelievable!" If Zane didn't know about magic, he would have been curious yet weary of seeing things move without someone orchestrating it all. Zane explored the office, enjoying the tastefully decorated space with garland, wreaths, and artisically placed hanging lights. The warmth came from the fireplace with stockings hanging on it. Next to the fireplace was a Christmas tree decorated in red, white, and silver. Next to the tree was a couch that looked so comfortable. Zane almost wanted to walk over and take a long nap since he hardly slept the night before, but stopped himself.

A bright smile crossed his lips as he took in more of the office space and was about to kneel and play with the train that had banged against his foot, but paused when the scent of cinnamon and gingerbread cookies wafted under his nose. Zane felt as if he were being pulled into a dream of his own desires. The place gave off a childlike but elegant air that didn't take away from the fact that it was a business and not a playground. With all the holiday cheer spread before him, Zane hadn't heard any Christmas music or seen anyone sitting at the receptionist's desk. Just as the thought crossed his mind, a door to the left opened, and a handsome man with flaming-red hair walked out.

He was as tall as Zane but not as muscular as he was, even though he could tell the man was an elf. He had a bright smile that could be called charming, but to Zane, it was annoying, especially when he noticed the redhead wasn't alone.

"Thank you, Havar," Frost said, grinning at the redhead.

Zane rubbed his chest when he felt it itch with an unknown feeling he could not describe.

"Come on, Frost. You know I would do anything for you." He chuckled and draped an arm over the petite elf's shoulders, who was staring up at him endearingly. "If only you'd give me the chance to show you just how good I can be to you."

Hearing that, the hairs on Zane's body bristled, and his wolf growled and paced in irritation. Without thinking about the consequences of his actions, Zane moved quickly and grabbed Frost by the hand, pulling him into his arms.

"Mine," he growled, glaring at the redhead in challenge.

FROST WAS SHOCKED when he was pulled from Havar's arms and was crushed against a hard chest. He was about to push the person away but stopped because of the most alluring scent and knew exactly who it was. Zane Blood-Moon. Even though they had only touched each other briefly, Frost had imprinted the man's scent on himself. Frost consciously leaned in close, taking it another breath. For his part, Zane tightened his arms around Frost, making him feel safe.

Frost's throat rolled, pressing down the purr that threatened to escape. To be held tenderly by his mate was not something Frost had seen happening. Christmas music filled with love suddenly started playing throughout the office. But Frost ignored it and basked in the moment. He wanted to stay there and never leave. However, it was impossible, no matter how much he wanted to remain in the man's arms.

"Who the fuck are you?" Frost heard Havar ask. Frost knew he should say something, but he wanted to listen to what Zane had to say.

"Are you deaf? I said mine," Zane stressed.

Havar tsked. "And what does the fuck does that mean?"

Frost waited for Zane to respond, but he said nothing else. The only sound was the music in the office that was magically queued to Frost's emotions. The songs had quickly changed, no longer playing happy Christmas music but chaotic, heart-pounding tunes showing how Frost felt the longer he waited for Zane to respond to Havar's question. The whole magical-music thing hadn't been his idea, but Bronwyn's. She thought the clients would either be confused or get a kick out of it if they figured out what was happening.

Taking a deep breath, he stepped out of Zane's hold. "Mister Blood-Moon, Bronwyn had to leave the office for a few minutes. You're free to wait or leave a message."

Frost turned to Havar and smiled. "Come to my office, and we can discuss the details of what we talked about earlier."

Ignoring the tall werewolf, Frost started walking to his office but was stopped by the man's words. "Is that all you have to say to me?"

Frost turned to face him. "What does *mine* mean?" Zane opened his mouth, but no sound came out, and Frost shook his head in disappointment. "As I expected. You want to claim someone but can't even say the word. You've already rejected me once. Why did I overthink this little display of attention? Goodbye, Mister Blood-Moon."

Frost walked by the man, with Havar following him, and this time, Zane didn't stop him. When he got to his office, Frost closed his door and took a few deep breaths. "Why did he have to show up today?"

"Who is he?" Havar asked.

Frost looked at the redheaded elf. "Forget about him. Let's discuss the changes for the upcoming Anderson wedding."

Havar said nothing for a few minutes and stared at him. They had been friends for a few years, and although Havar had asked him out countless times, the man was not lacking lovers. However, he was more of a friend than anything else. He saw the look on his friend's face and knew that no matter what he said, Havar wouldn't give up.

"Fuck, Hav, do you have to go into this right now?"

"No," Havar answered. "I've already figured it out. He's your mate. So I guess I've lost my shot."

Frost smiled uncomfortably, not saying anything.

Havar chuckled, walked over, and pulled him into a hug. Frost wanted to pull away. Normally he would be fine with Havar's touch, but things had changed since Zane entered his life. Yet he couldn't step away. He was yearning for an intimate touch, even if it was from a friend.

"From your words, I don't think he rejected you. Maybe he's confused or has extenuating circumstances he's not ready to share. But I'm sure everything will work out." He leaned back and looked down at Frost. "I'm just sad that I've lost my chance."

"I'm sorry," Frost whispered.

"Why are you apologizing? It's a blessing to find your mate."

Yeah, but what happens when your mate rejects you? Frost thought but nodded his head instead. "Yes, it is."

"All right, let's get to work," he said, changing the topic. "If I'm going to be a partner in the company, I need to up my game."

Havar had agreed to be partners in F.W. Events. Once Bronwyn agreed, Frost would make the necessary changes, but for now, they had work to do.

FROST SNAPPED his gaze away from Havar when he heard Zane's voice. *Why is he still here?*

"I thought you left," Frost said.

"Apparently," Zane sneered, then he turned to Bronwyn. "Send me the information, and I will meet you whenever you're ready" With one last scathing look at Frost, he left his office.

"Fuck," Frost said and stepped away from Havar.

"I'm sorry about that, Frost," Havar said.

Frost shook his head. "It's not your fault. Things between me and him are complicated." Frost sighed and pulled out his phone when it vibrated in his pants pocket, seeing that his brother had sent him a message.

"His first mate died and friends say he decided not to take another. Or fall in love, for that matter."

Reading Nyx's message, Frost was crushed and mentally cursed, feeling a little wronged. How was he supposed to know Zane had a mate before? He needed to speak with his brother. Walking back into his office, Frost called his brother, who picked up on their first ring.

"How did his mate die? How long ago was this? How did you find out?"

Nyx chuckled. "You know I have my sources. I can find out anything. As for his mate, she died in a car crash. The other driver was drunk and lost his life. Arizona was human, and it was a few years ago. Arizona Ravensong Hart. She never took his last night after they got mated."

Frost's brows creased together. "Was she part of the Ravensong bloodline?"

"Yes," Nyx answered.

Frost knew of the Ravensong coven; they were known to be strong witches and warlocks with covens all over the world. He recalled hearing about Arizona Ravensong, a beautiful model who had both men and women proposing marriage to her, yet she turned them all down. Now he knew why.

So they were mates. Fuck.

He also remembered when Arizona announced that she

was taking some time away from the spotlight and was gone for roughly a year and a half. It coincided with the time Zane had quit being a model. It was some years later when news of her death shocked the world.

"There's one more thing," Nyx said.

Frost didn't need to hear what his brother had to say. He could already guess.

"They had a daughter."

Frost sat in his chair, unsure what to think or say. He had thought the man had rejected him because he didn't want a mate, but he was still heartbroken after losing his first.

"Thanks for telling me," Frost said to Nyx.

"Come see me after you get off work. We'll have a meal together," Nyx ordered softly.

"Hmm..." he said in a noncommittal way. Truthfully, he wasn't in the mood to see anyone. He had already embarrassed himself twice in front of Zane Blood-Moon. He needed time to come to grips with his mate's rejection. *Maybe I should go away for a bit.*

CHAPTER FIVE

Zane got home later that night feeling quite irritated, not because of the company's troubles but due to a certain fae. The image of seeing Winterbourne in the redhead's arms was repeated in his mind for the rest of his day. He roughly pulled his tie off his neck, growling, then threw it on the kitchen counter, growing more irate when his frustration wasn't eased.

How dare he let someone else hold him? Wasn't he ready to call us mates? And why the fuck do I have to say what mine means? And who said I rejected him?

Zane marched over to the fridge, roughly pulling it open. He grabbed a beer, and just as he was about to pop the top, a throat cleared behind him. He looked over his shoulder, and his gaze landed on Megan. Zane had completely forgotten she was going to be here. He put the beer back and closed the doors.

"Hi, Megan," he said, as he turned to greet her. Shoving his hands in his pockets, Zane leaned against the fridge doors, feeling as if he needed their support.

"Bad day?" she asked.

"I've had better. Thanks for helping me out with Hannah today. I hope she didn't give you any trouble."

"Not at all. It's a pleasure to take care of her," Megan said, giving him a shy glance. Megan Lord was a vision of stunning beauty, her moderately long, luscious brown locks cascading gracefully to frame a face that perfectly complemented her light brown complexion. Standing next to him, her gaze effortlessly met his chest, and her captivating brown eyes emanated warmth, making anyone fortunate enough to be the focus of her gaze feel an undeniable connection. And, of course, her radiant and brilliantly dazzling smile added an extra layer of charm to her already enchanting presence.

However, Zane had never seen Megan as anything besides a friend or a little sister. They had been friends since Megan and her family moved into the neighborhood. He could only assume what Hannah was getting at earlier that morning and prayed his little girl wasn't getting any idea of playing matchmaker.

"Do you want to talk about what has upset you so much? I don't mind listening," Megan asked, and somehow, she had gotten closer to him during his mindscape. "Maybe I could help."

"Ah...no, I'm good," he said quickly as a thought came to him, and he stepped to the side. "Can you do me another favor?"

She seemed a bit disappointed for some odd reason; however, she quickly smiled. "Sure, what is it?"

"Mind staying with Hannah for a couple of hours. I'm going to go for a run. It will help me a great deal."

"Okay," Megan whispered.

"Thanks." Without further delay, Zane ran upstairs, changed into sweats, and headed out the backdoor without saying another word to Hannah. Even on a half-moonlit night, there was enough magic for Zane to let his wolf experience some freedom. He jogged to the depths of the woods not far from his home and stripped, then shifted into a large gray wolf with deep, soulful brown eyes.

Thanks to the Pryde sect, there was much forested land where a rogue like himself could run and hunt without impeding on their property. Zane closed his eyes and let the cold air wash over him. Slowly, he opened them and, lifting one paw after the other, started running, letting his mind wander as a burst of soft female laughter reached his ear, and he reminisced of the days when he'd shifted in front of Arizona and the games they played. He missed those times and often wished he could bring those moments back.

The laughter died down as a sweet voice seemed to whisper in the wind. *"It's time to move on, Zane. Give love one more chance."*

Before he could register what was happening, an image emerged in his mind—a temperamental fae with snow-white hair and large colorful wings flapping behind him, them being playful and later making love under the moon and stars. Zane stopped mid-run, gasping for breath.

What the fuck? If I'm thinking about mating him, will I be able to let him go?

A FEW DAYS LATER, Zane drove through the large wrought-iron gates, whistling in awe as the mansion, or he should call it a castle, came into view. There was a large marble fountain in the middle of the manicured garden. Zane marveled at the double-wide staircase leading up to the large stained-glass French doors.

"When Bronwyn said she had a venue, I wasn't expecting it to be this grand."

The mansion wasn't far from the city; although he hadn't known the place existed, it wasn't hard to find. Zane had been out of the country trying to stop his company from crumbling since someone was hell-bent on taking him down, but he had been in contact with Bronwyn. In his case, most people would have canceled the celebration party long ago, but his employees had also made the company what it was today.

Zane wished he knew what he'd done to place a bullseye on him and his company. He was glad they hadn't attacked his reputation. Yet, even with everything happening, he couldn't help but think about Frost Winterbourne. Going out of the country or even going for nightly runs in his wolf wasn't getting the man out of his thoughts. During his conversations with Bronwyn, he often wanted to ask about Winterbourne's wellbeing, but he was uncertain what the fae had told the witch about their relationship. She was still courteous, but he could hear a slight annoyance in her tone whenever they spoke.

Maybe I should give love a second chance like the wind advised. Fuck, am I crazy?

While away, Zane thought long and hard about his situation and admitted that his heart fluttered madly each time the fae crossed his mind. Not only that, but he knew he had been too close-minded about mating. Especially since Hannah was a child, he'd taught her the ways of their world and how special it was to find the ones the gods had designed for them. And it was only a matter of time and fate before she saw them.

Have I been so closed-hearted and minded that I've forgotten my teachings?

The goddesses of fate would never let him go without a mate for long. And if he continued to ignore the pull toward Winterbourne, he didn't know what could happen. Zane realized he'd fucked up royally if the fae was carrying the notion that he had rejected him as a mate.

Sure, he was naïve in thinking that their mating bond would break after a while, the less time they spent together, but maybe that only worked when mated to a human and not a supernatural. Zane parked his car in the driveway and stared at the magnificent home, wondering who it belonged to. The door opened, and Zane was surprised when Frost walked out.

He leaned forward, gripping the steering wheel, observing the man who'd occupied most of his thoughts while away on his trip. The man was good-looking from head to toe and, honestly, Zane's type, with his height and toned body that fit quite well in the dark blue suit he had on.

A few buttons on his black shirt were undone, showing off his light complexion and clear chest. Zane unconsciously licked his lips, wanting to trail kisses and marks on his skin. He couldn't help loosening his tie and unbuttoning a couple of buttons on his shirt.

Zane smiled, liking his hair pulled into a tight bun neatly twisted on the top of his head but became a little concerned the fae wasn't wearing a jacket since the weather had gotten colder in his absence, prompting him to get out of the car, not forgetting to grab his outer coat and walk over to the elf who had met him halfway.

"I thought I was meeting Bronwyn." Zane mentally winced at his stupidity. It wasn't the first thing he wanted to say. He initially wanted to show his gentlemanly side and offer the elf his coat.

Shit, I keep fucking up with him. Zane went to speak, but the other man was quicker.

"Hello to you too, Mister Blood-Moon." His voice was soft yet cold, devoid of any emotion.

Fuck, he's still mad at me. But I can't blame him. It seems I'm going to have to tread very carefully.

"How are you?" Zane asked.

Frost stared at him for a few seconds, then turned away and entered the house. "Bronwyn was called away by her family, so I'm going solo for a few days. I hope you don't mind that I'm the one to show you around the Eclipse."

"The Eclipse?"

"Yes, that's the name of the mansion. Built in 1865, it got renovated and updated over the years a few times over, but the owners kept the original design, or the last one did, at least." He stopped and turned to look at Zane. "I hope it meets your standards. We have a lot of work to do and not enough time to look at other places." He waved a hand around. "We can accommodate any change you require, as long as it doesn't demolish the home."

Zane looked around the home, and even though they were in the foyer, it was quite grand, with two large staircases. A larger, partially decorated but lit Christmas tree stood regally under the stairs, or maybe because it was in front of the stained glass window, giving off an elegant atmosphere.

On the left side was the sitting room that was decorated in all white, which went well with the stormy-blue-painted walls, cathedral ceilings, and wide windows that would let in the sunlight during the day. He could even picture himself in his wolf, sitting beside the fireplace, basking in the moon while his lover ran his slim, beautiful fingers through his fur.

This place far exceeded his expectations, even after only seeing a small portion. He wanted to see more.

"Come on, let me show you around," Frost said.

ZANE NODDED AND FOLLOWED FROST, who took him to the open kitchen painted in soft cream with marble countertops and an island breakfast table. More large windows surrounded the room, letting in natural light.

Zane moved over to the window and scanned the backyard, which had a garden and a pond with salvinia plants floating on the surface. The home was tastefully decorated for the holiday and had plenty of rooms to hold his fairy tale ball.

"It's lovely here," Zane whispered.

"Yes, it is." Winterbourne's soft voice came from behind him. His tone had many more emotions than he had heard in a long time.

Zane looked over his shoulder. The fae turned and walked away as he was about to say more.

"Follow me; there's more. I want to show you the room we'll section off for guests who might have had too much to drink," he said hurriedly.

Being in the fae's presence, it had become apparent that Zane couldn't break the bond between them. It would be idiotic to say he wasn't attracted to the man. Zane watched the fae walk ahead of him and shook his head disappointedly. He was fighting a losing battle. He wanted to talk about more than just the house, but the man kept him at a distance. Zane knew it was his own fault, but he still didn't like it. Sighing, Zane followed the fae and focused—or tried to anyway—as the fae showed him around the mansion.

When they were face to face, he couldn't help watching how his pretty lips moved when he spoke or when he moistened them after talking for a long time. Zane purposely made the man walk in front of him so he could watch his legs and cute ass move in sync.

It didn't help his plight that instead of mint and snow, a pleasurable scent of peaches with a hint of vanilla trailed behind the fae, driving Zane crazy and making him want his favorite dessert, a fresh-out-of-the-oven slice of peach cobbler with vanilla ice cream on top. He licked his lips, wanting to take a bite in that instant.

Or maybe it would be better to eat them both simultaneously. An image of licking warm peach juices with the ice cream from the fae's body was now etched in his thoughts. He wanted to hear Frost's sighs and moans as he gobbled every inch of the man up. Zane was sure he would have more salacious images playing in his mind during his nightly run.

"So, what do you think?"

Zane heard the question but wasn't sure what he was being asked. He quickly blinked and cleared his throat, looking away from the beautiful fae. Zane had been so lost in his thoughts that he hadn't realized they had returned to the kitchen. He was a bit surprised there was a fresh pot of coffee sitting on the island, a teapot and cups, along with varieties of cookies and cupcakes. Zane remembered it wasn't there the first time they were in the kitchen.

"Where did all the goodies come from?" he asked, pointing to the setup.

Frost smiled. And it was mesmerizing. "I had the butler take care of it."

"Butler?" Zane had the notion that they were the only

two in the house. He also didn't recall seeing or getting a scent that someone else was there.

"Oh," Zane said.

"Would you like something to drink while we talk?" the fae asked.

Zane nodded. "Tea," he said. "But I can get it." He moved to stand next to Winterbourne, but the fae backed away and busied himself with making Zane's tea.

"Have a seat, I'll bring it over to you," Frost told him.

Seeing he had no other options, Zane sighed and sat at the other end of the island, watching as the fae moved around the kitchen easily, seeming to know where everything was.

He may know the owner of the house. A terrible feeling lodged itself in the pit of Zane's stomach. *What if the owner tries to impress the fae by giving him unlimited use and access to his home? Would Winterbourne fall for it, and I'll lose my chance to get to know him because I flip-flopped on my emotions? Fuck, what the hell am I thinking?*

Zane wasn't sure how he knew, but he had a feeling that Winterbourne wouldn't be enchanted by anyone who wanted to throw money at him just because they could.

"Here you go."

"Thank you." Zane took the teacup with three different flavors of tea and the plate filled with a couple of cupcakes and a few cookies.

"I didn't exactly know what you liked, so..." he said with a shrug.

Zane smiled. "It's okay, I'm not picky." He picked up a chocolate chip cookie, taking a big bite out of it, not taking his eyes off the fae. It wasn't the peach cobbler he'd been fantasizing about, but seeing the cute blush on his cheeks made up for it.

Winterbourne cleared his throat. "So you didn't answer my earlier question?"

"And that is?" Zane set the cookie down and prepared his tea.

"What do you think of the Eclipse for your office party?"

From what he'd seen and remembered, he liked the place very much. It would work well with the theme he had in mind.

"I like it," Zane said after a few minutes. "Mister Winterbourne, this is truly a marvelous home."

"Very well," Winterbourne nodded. "And please call me Frost."

"Only if you take the liberty of calling me Zane."

Frost didn't respond and simply held out his hand with his palm facing up, and a blue sparkling light with a hint of gold appeared above it. Zane could feel the magic in the room; it was soft and comforting, unlike when he had been around magic users who left him annoyed.

Once the light disappeared, a file was left behind. Before Zane could say anything, Frost pushed it in front of him.

"Bronwyn came up with some ideas that would work. Give them a once-over and get back to us with what you think." He stood and waved his hand, and out of the corner of his eye, something zoomed by him and was caught by Frost, and Zane realized it was the man's coat that he was shrugging on.

"Stay as long as you like. Look around again if you need to."

"Wait!" Zane hurriedly stood, realizing Frost was leaving. *I can't let that happen.* "Are you leaving?"

"Yes," Frost said, fixing his coat collar. "I have a prior engagement."

Fuck, I didn't expect to see him today, but now that he's here, why is he rushing off?

"But what about..." Zane felt a bit tongue-tied and simply pointed to the folder on the table. "I thought you'd help me decide."

Zane stared at him imploringly; however, the adorable fae remained cold-faced. If anyone saw Zane trying to look pitiful right now, they wouldn't believe the man in the boardroom was a hardass and intelligent man.

Zane mentally remarked again about how royally he had fucked up. The minute he knew he and Frost were mates, he should have explained things, and he needed to fix things between them, even though he did not know what he was going to say, but for now, he had to keep the young fae tethered to him. Zane was going to try another tactic when Frost spoke.

"Is this how you conduct business, Mister Blood-Moon?"

"And what do you mean?" Zane asked, playing the fool. "And why do you call me by my last name? It's Zane, remember?"

"I only call people I consider friends by their first name," Frost told him with a stony face.

Zane placed a hand over his chest. "Ouch, that really stings, but I guess I deserve it."

Not even a crack in his mask. Zane had hoped to get a reaction to his last statement, but nothing. *Fuck, I didn't think he'd be this hard even to make him smile.*

"Good night, Mister Blood-Moon." He turned to leave, but Zane lightly grabbed his elbow and said the first thing that came out of his mouth.

"I didn't reject you." He released Frost as the man turned to face him, giving him the first look of interest since they met that day. Zane ran his fingers through his hair. "I know that's what you thought. Saying I'm sorry won't take away the way I made you feel."

"Why are you saying this to me now when I told myself to move on?"

"So that's why you've been giving me the cold shoulder?" Oddly, that made Zane happy.

"But you apologizing to me changes nothing," Frost said. "You still don't want a mate."

"I thought I didn't."

CHAPTER SIX

Frost felt his insides quiver hearing the doubt in Zane's voice, but he did not let himself believe there was hope at the end of the tunnel. He stared at the handsome man who seemed a bit exhausted, pulling on Frost's heartstrings. He didn't even want to think of how cute the other man had acted a couple of minutes earlier, almost causing him to break his mask.

I should have let Bronwyn reschedule.

But that wouldn't have worked since he knew how constrained they were. Even with magic, they needed time to put everything together.

A few hours ago, he had wanted to kill Bronwyn when she burst into his office and begged him to take over her meeting with Zane because she had a family emergency.

Frost would have thought she was up to something, like trying to play matchmaker after he had explained the whole mating thing to her. Frost knew Bronwyn did not like Zane for rejecting him, but she was more worried about the birth of her nephew.

Bronwyn's sister, Jadis, was six months pregnant and

had unexpectedly gone into early labor. So, the entire family had gathered at the hospital, hoping to support the soon-to-be parents.

Even after knowing about the man's first mate, Frost had been on pins and needles about meeting with Zane.

During the days they hadn't seen each other, Frost had much time to think and decided to let Zane Blood-Moon go. No matter how good-looking the man was, Frost had never thrown himself at a man and did not plan on holding onto someone who did not want him—but hearing what Zane said piqued his interest.

"What do you mean by that?" Frost asked.

"It means I'm trying to figure out what *mine* means."

"OH," Frost whispered.

"Is that all you have to say?" His reaction didn't put off Zane, but he was hoping for more.

"I'm not sure what to say."

"Say you'll listen to my explanation."

"Okay," Frost said.

Zane smiled, stepped behind him, and reached out to take his coat but stopped himself. "Since we have the perfect setting." He pointed to the table with the snacks laid out for them. "Come back to the table. Sit back down, and we can talk."

Frost looked at him over his shoulders for a few moments before he sighed, nodded, and then walked back over to the table and sat down, pouring himself a fresh cup of tea.

Zane mentally thanked whatever god was paying attention to his plight. Although he did not know what would happen afterward, he couldn't let the fae walk away without knowing the truth. He placed Frost's coat on the island, then joined him at the table. They stared at each other, and Zane couldn't help but mentally remark how handsome the fae was.

"Do you plan on speaking or staring at me all night?"

"Why can't I do both?"

"You're free to do as you please, but I wasn't lying when I said I had a prior engagement."

Zane cleared his throat and sat up. "Damn, you're kind of hard on a guy. Next time I'm negotiating a deal, I'll bring you with me, and you can scare the board into giving in to me."

The fae cracked a smile for the first time, and Zane's heart fluttered seeing the reaction.

"You should smile more," he commented. "It brightens up your face."

"And I like the way you grovel."

"You go straight for the throat, don't you?

"You're not the first person to tell me that," he said, then smirked. "But don't expect me to change."

"I wouldn't dare ask you to," Zane said with a smile as it slowly slipped off his face. He wanted to stall for a bit longer but knew he had to tell Frost something.

Truthfully, he had spoken little about Arizona since her death, not even to Hannah. He did not hide Arizona from her and tried his best to answer any question she had about her mother. But this would be the first time he would bring her up without being prodded. The silence between them dragged, but it was comforting.

"I had a mate," he said, feeling his throat go tight, and he was thankful that Frost hadn't asked questions and allowed him to continue. "Arizona was the most beautiful woman I'd ever seen." He smiled. "We met on the catwalk in Paris."

Zane closed his eyes, and an image of Arizona flashed through his mind, of the elegant black-and-silver evening dress that had contoured her figure. But as quickly as the beautiful vision came, it changed to Zane getting the horrifying phone call and being told the terrible news. Instantly, Zane's eyes snapped open. Not wanting to relive that moment again, he was shocked when his hand was touched by warmth, slowly healing the pain in his heart. Zane swallowed, and his throat was parched, so he picked up his teacup, took large gulps, and then set the cup down with a shaky hand.

"She was killed by a drunk driver and it killed me that she died alone far away from me" He looked down at the hand on his, then back up at the other man. "Engine failure. It was one of the worst moments of my life." Zane took a deep breath. "I was so distraught after Arizona died that I made a vow not to find another mate. I didn't want to feel the pain of losing someone again." He grasped the fae's hand in his. "That day in your office when we touched, I was shocked and didn't know what to think. But my careless action hurt you, and I'm sorry."

Zane's gaze returned to their hands, and he remarked that they fit well together. "I'm not sure what will happen between us, Frost." He raised his eyes to meet the other's gaze. "And I know I might be asking for too much, but can you give me some time to figure out my feelings? I know she's never coming back, but I closed my heart to love again and focused on what I thought mattered. Since meeting you, I haven't been able to get you out of my thoughts. It's been a while since I've been with anyone, so give me some time to get to know you. Don't close your heart to me." Zane stared at the man with pitiful eyes, hoping he would understand.

"Okay," Frost said after a few minutes, bringing a bright smile to Zane's face.

"Thank you."

Frost shook his head, releasing Zane's hand, and stood. "There's no need to thank me. I'm doing this for selfish reasons."

Zane's brows furrowed. "What do you mean?"

"This might sound crass, but I refuse to share you with a dead person," he said, shrugging off his outer coat and slinging on the back of the chair. "Because once we're mated, I need to be the only lover in your heart."

Zane's eyes widened before he barked out a laugh. "You truly say how you feel."

"It's one of my better qualities," the fae said with a saucy wink. "All right, let's get to work."

"Work? Don't you want to hear more about Arizona?" As much as it would hurt to talk about her, Zane figured Frost would have questions. He also wanted to tell him about Hannah, but maybe it was too soon to say, "H*ey, I have a kid*." He'd kept his daughter's existence from the media, not wanting her to be scrutinized because of who her father was.

"Not yet. As intrigued as I am to hear about her, I can see how hard it is for you even to mention her name," he whispered. "So I will wait until you can."

Zane reached over and grabbed his hands, clenching them. "Thank you."

"I told you, don't thank me. This is me being selfish."

"I didn't think faes were the selfish kind," Zane remarked. "I've always heard you lot had a giving nature."

"You're thinking of elves. Those are the selfless bastards

who'd give up their left arm if someone begged them." He leaned across the table seductively. Zane couldn't help but feel trapped in a good way. Frost placed a finger under Zane's chin, pulling him forward until their faces were a breath apart. "My kind, however, are mischievous, flirtatious." He licked his lips, and Zane's eyes couldn't help but follow the motion. "We're also very territorial."

Zane swallowed and was sure that even the neighbors ten miles away could hear it. "Good...good to know."

There was a seductive bubble around them, and it felt like the man had him trapped in a spider web. But just as the thought crossed his mind, it popped, and he was being unraveled. Frost leaned back in his chair, looking as if nothing had happened. It took Zane a few more seconds to compose himself. Sitting back in his chair, he ran a hand over his shirt and took a couple of deep breath feeling the need for more air in his lungs. He was about to stand and get a cup of water, but he froze when he realized he was about to embarrass the fuck out of himself. His dick was hard and tenting his pants. Glancing down at his crotch, Zane was a little shocked.

Fuck, when the hell did that happen? Not that Zane hadn't had an erection since his mate died. It had popped up out of nowhere, making him feel like a pubescent teenager. Since meeting Frost Winterbourne, Zane could say in one breath that his life had been a whirlwind.

"I think you should go with this package."

Frost's voice pulled him from his thoughts, making him look at the man, recalling he said something about work. Not wanting to give anything away, Zane stretched out a hand for the file and saw the words scavenger hunt on the paper. "I like it," he said after a few minutes of scanning the documents. He honestly did not know what the fuck he'd read; he was just waiting for his dick to settle down.

"Okay."

Frost took the file from him and chewed on his bottom lip, and Zane had to look away so that he didn't get turned on or do something like grab the man and kiss him until they were both breathless. Zane could readily admit that his emotions were in turmoil. On the one hand, he wanted to take the fae into his arms; on the other, he felt doing so would betray his love for Arizona.

"Take a look at the menu options available. The good thing is you have a couple of days to decide," Frost said seriously, not looking up at him.

"I'll do that. Anything else?"

"I'll have my people work the scavenger hunt and get the invitations out. If there are business associates you want to attend this, send us their information, and we'll take care of it. Of course, we'll send you the invitation proofs so you can agree."

Zane knew the business was good at their job, but he had no idea they were so hands-on, or maybe this was something special just for him, which made Zane puff up his chest. "Do you do this for all your clients?"

"Mhmm, it's part of the package," he responded without raising his head.

"Oh," Zane said, hoping he didn't sound as if his bubble didn't burst.

"Also, if there's anything you want changed or added to the house, let me know," Frost informed him.

"Why would I want to change anything? I like the way it is. I normally don't like large homes, but I wouldn't mind living here."

"Really?" Frost instantly raised his head, and Zane got to stare into his pretty blue jeweled eyes.

"Yeah. I feel bad that I get to use it just for a party and nothing else."

Frost smiled. "You never know. Maybe one day you'll use it for another party or something more significant."

"It's possible, but I wouldn't mind living here rather than using it for any kind of event." Zane could see Hannah playing in the large backyard. He'd turn one bedroom into her playroom and another into an office so he could work from home more often. He wasn't sure what he'd do with the rest of the house, but the place was big enough to turn it into a bed-and-breakfast if he went the business route.

Shit, if I like it this much, I might as well buy it.

"Do you have the owner's information handy?"

"Why?" Frost asked, tilting his head.

Zane looked around the kitchen and noted that it was his favorite place in the house.

"I'm interested in buying it once the ball..."

"It's not for sale," Frost cut him off before he could say more.

Zane looked at him irritatedly. "How the hell do you know that?" Zane didn't like to be cut off.

"Because it was a gift."

"A gift."

"Yes, it was given to me by someone special." He smiled as if reliving a wonderful memory, but it was nudging at Zane's jealousy, especially after his next sentence. "I saw it in a magazine, and *he* bought it for me."

He? Who the fuck is he? Zane wanted to ask but knew he couldn't. He hadn't claimed the fae yet, so he had to smile like an idiot and eat his belly full of jealousy.

"Oh," was all he could say in the end.

Zane knew how much a home of this magnitude cost, and the fact that some dude shelled out the money for it just because Frost liked it made even an alpha like Zane doubt his confidence.

What can I give him in the future that would compare to this? Fuck, I'm going to have to step up my game.

FROST DID NOT KNOW what Zane was going through, but by the tense expression on his face, he was in deep thought. Although he had said he'd give Zane time to get his emotions together, it didn't mean he'd sit idly by and let the man string him along. Frost planned to be proactive but not forceful. Frost had to believe that they would be together soon, and it wasn't wishful thinking on his part.

"So, you and the guy who brought the house are close?"

Frost smiled. "You could say that." He was about to tell Zane that his brother Nyx bought him the house as a birthday present, but when he heard the jealous tinge in the man's voice, he figured he'd hold on to that small detail for later.

As aloof as Zane thought he was acting, Frost had noticed the wolf's every action, from letting him walk in front of him to trying to keep him from leaving when he should have been gone a long time ago. He was supposed to meet Nyx for dinner, but if Frost knew his brother, the man was still working and would call when he was ready to eat.

"How close?" Zane asked.

Frost put his elbow on the table and rested his chin on his hand, gazing into the werewolf's eyes that seemed to be blazing with fire. "Why do you need to know all of that information? As far as I know, we're just in the getting-to-know-you stage."

Zane went to speak but was interrupted by his ringing cellphone sitting on the table. Frost quickly glanced down and saw the name *Baby Girl* and took a guess that it was his daughter, but he didn't give anything away since he wasn't supposed to know about her. But it also made Frost wonder why Zane hadn't told him about her.

Maybe he's not ready to reveal everything. Then I'll give him time.

"Sorry, I have to take this."

"It's no problem."

Zane smiled, grabbed his cellphone, and stood, walking over to the window. He spoke in low tones, and to give him some privacy, Frost sent a quick message to Bronwyn and then his brother, who called him right away.

"What do you mean you're with Blood-Moon," Nyx questioned, making Frost roll his eyes.

"Working, what do you think?" Frost sighed.

"He rejected you."

"He's paying me to do a job, Nyx."

"You don't need the money. I can..."

"Stop, look, I'll be at your office in a bit. Then we can go to dinner, and I'll explain everything."

"You better," Nyx growled.

They hung up just as Zane came back over to him. "I'm sorry, but I need to cut our time short. I have to take care of something."

"It's all right." Frost stood and grabbed his coat, shrugging it on. "I need to leave as well. Contact Bronwyn in a day or two; she'll take good care of you." Frost was about to leave, but Zane stopped him.

"Thanks," he said.

"For what?"

"The use of your home and for listening to me."

"No thanks are needed."

Frost stared at him, and before he could do anything, Zane moved closer to him. "I'll be a little busy this week, but can we meet for lunch or dinner?"

Frost smiled. "I don't see why not. Call me when you have a break in your schedule."

Zane smiled, leaned down, and kissed him on the forehead, sending a sweet warmth to Frost's toes. He clenched his fingers together to stop himself from touching the spot.

"Thanks once again," Zane said, stepping back and collecting the papers, and he left, with Frost standing in the same spot, unable to move.

Fuck, with just one small gesture, I'm rendered motionless. Damn, that man could be my undoing.

CHAPTER SEVEN

In the days that followed since their talk at the Eclipse, things went smoothly for Frost. He met with new clients who wanted events planned in the new year and continued to make the final touches on Lisa and Mark's wedding. And there was a lot of progress between him and Zane.

They hadn't seen each other since the night of their talk at the Eclipse because Zane had to leave for an impromptu business trip to Italy, so their lunch date was postponed. But they'd been texting each other a few times a day. Frost smiled, scrolling through his phone and recalling their conversations.

Zane: What's your favorite color?"

Frost didn't even think why Zane would ask that question and answered immediately.

Frost: Red.

Zane: I didn't see that one coming. I thought it would be blue or something. Aren't you going to ask me about mine?"

Frost: I already know what it is.

Zane: Really? Then what is it?

Frost: The color of the moon when it's at its fullest.

Zane: Wow, you're right. So, what is your favorite breakfast meal?

Frost: Do you seriously need to know that?"

Zane: Of course. By chance, what if I want to make you breakfast?"

Frost: Will we ever get to that point?"

There wasn't an instant response, but that was how their conversations went, with them getting to know each other. Frost looked forward to Zane's text each day. He woke up to one and got another one before falling asleep at night.

Frost wanted to ask why Zane had gone out of town and if it concerned his company's troubles. Frost had found out his brother had taken his words to heart and started going after Zane's company. But after he explained everything to Nyx, his big brother promised to fix things with Zane's company. He would also back off and let things between him and Zane play out.

"Hey, boss, I need your help," Bronwyn said, barging into his office.

Frost set his phone down face first and looked up at his friend. "What's up?"

"I can't decide on something for Blood-Moon's party."

"Why don't you call him and ask him?"

"He's not answering his phone, so I assume he's in a meeting. Besides, he said if he can't be reached, I should ask your opinion," she said with a shrug.

That shocked Frost; Zane hadn't said anything to him. "Why or when did he say that?"

"Just before he left. We went over everything for his party. By the way, I've been meaning to ask you: Since when have we personally sent out the invitations for our clients? Usually, we let them do it. Do you know how long it would have taken me without magic to stuff over three hundred envelopes?"

"It just popped into my head. Anyway, what do you need help deciding?"

"Outside wine bar? I was wondering if we should have one or not. We have that big backyard. I don't see why we should leave it out of the fun."

"You're right. Set up a floating tent with a few comfortable chairs as well. Top-shelf alcohol is a must. Hopefully, we could get a couple of clientele out of this gig."

"Sounds good," she said, and Frost reached for his cellphone to continue reading through his messages with Zane but froze when he noticed Bronwyn hadn't left and raised his gaze to meet hers.

"Is there something else?"

"What are you reading?" She leaned across his desk, trying to see what he was doing. Frost pressed his phone to his chest, blocking the screen from her view.

"Stop nosing around in my business and get to work."

"I can't believe you're keeping secrets from me. I thought we were best friends."

"Stop trying to play the guilt card." He waved his hand, shooing her away. "Go on, get out of here."

"Okay, answer one question, and I'll go." Frost sighed and nodded. "Is it from Zane?"

Frost smiled. "Yes, we've been texting each other for the past few days."

She quirked a brow. "Not calling. In this day and age, you guys could do more than that."

"We're taking things slow. I told you about his first mate. And I don't mind the whole text thing. We're still at the beginning stages."

"I see," she said. "So, how slow are we talking?"

Frost was about to answer, but there was a knock at his office door before it was opened, and Frost's eyes widened in surprise when Zane's face came into view. Frost was about to jump out of his seat and greet the man, but Bronwyn touched his shoulder, stopping him from moving.

"Mister Blood-Moon, it's rude to enter without getting a response. What if we were in a meeting?"

"Are you? Because I can come back later."

Bronwyn sighed. "No, I was just leaving." She looked at Frost and mumbled low enough for Frost's ear, "Slow, huh? It seems to me you're about to jump out of your seat at the sight of him."

"Get out," Frost whispered.

She chuckled as she walked out of the room, and Frost slowly got up and moved over to Zane.

"She's a loyal pe...person."

"We've been through a lot. I thought you were still in Italy."

"I left right after I finished my business last night. I just landed."

Frost quirked his brow. "And I'm the first person you came to see?"

"I would like to say that you were, but I had to make a stop before I came to see you to fulfill the promise I made to take you on a lunch date. I'm not one to go back on my word. Well, when it comes to certain things."

Frost understood his meaning and could only assume that during their time apart, Zane really took some time to think things through.

"So, are you free to have lunch with me?"

"I am," Frost responded.

"Then let's go."

ZANE GRABBED Frost's coat and dropped it over his shoulder. "What are you in the mood for?"

"Would it be off-putting if I said Italian?"

"Not at all."

Zane had spent the past few days eating hotel takeout and going from one meeting to another and shamefully did not have time to explore Italy. His company was doing better than ever. He still hadn't found out who was trying to take down his company, but one day, he woke up and his stocks had opened the market on a high, almost breaking the needle.

His impromptu out-of-town trip was so that he could buy a new technology company. But after one day of being gone, he wanted to return to his daughter and Frost. Zane thought it was time for them to meet. And during the slight breaks when he didn't have meetings, he'd sent a few texts to Frost, hoping to get to know him. Zane knew he could call, but he had a feeling that if he'd heard the man's smooth voice, he'd have been home quicker, not getting any work done.

While getting to know Frost, Zane had to admit he had been going through the motions of being but not living. Maybe that was why the gods had given him another mate, and he realized no one was alone. Crazy as it might sound, Zane had thought that Arizona also had a guiding hand with him meeting Frost Winterbourne.

On a whim before heading out of the country, Zane had gone to the family cemetery. He'd sat in silence for almost an hour just staring at her picture before uttering the word goodbye. He didn't feel his heart breaking into pieces, nor did he experience any regret.

The place Arizona had left in his heart was still there, and he doubted it would ever go away, but there was enough room to let someone in. If he hadn't met Frost and they hadn't found out they were mates, maybe he would have stayed alone and watched Hannah grow up and find her own mate. But the gods and maybe Arizona took pity on his foolish thoughts and still gave him a mate whom he was close to rejecting.

"Did your business trip go all right?" Frost asked him, putting the menu to the side.

"It went well. I will open an international branch in the new year."

"So you'll be busy?"

"Somewhat, but I've turned the rest of the deal over to one of my most trusted advisors. But let's not talk shop." He reached for Frost's hand and steepled their fingers together. "I want to discuss us."

"Really?"

"Yes." He smiled. "I'm not saying I'm ready for us to jump into bed yet, but I don't want to keep us apart any longer."

"What are you saying?" Frost leaned forward and stared into Zane's eyes, making it hard for him to look away.

Zane raised the hand he was holding and brought it to his lips. "I've done a lot of thinking the past few days, and I know we're taking things slow. There are a couple of things I need to work out, but I'm ready to move forward."

Frost looked at him pensively. "Are you sure?"

"Yes," he answered. Zane looked down at their joined hands and slowly raised his gaze. "There was another reason I held back before. There's someone important in my life I want you to meet."

Zane reached into his jacket pocket and pulled out his

cellphone, unlocking it quickly. He sifted through his photo album and brought up his favorite picture of his daughter, then pushed his cellphone in front of Frost.

"This is Hannah, my daughter. I know I should have told you about her before or, fuck, asked you if you wanted kids, but I didn't want to bring her into this until I was sure of what I wanted."

Frost glanced down at the screen and then looked back up at him. "She's gorgeous, but she looks nothing like you," he said jokingly.

Zane smiled. "She gets her features from her mother."

"When I was younger," he said, "I think I was the only one in my friend circle who knew I wanted at least three kids." He looked up at Zane, smiling. "I want to meet her, but not before you're ready."

Zane brought Frost's hand to his lips and kissed his fingers. "Thank you for understanding. But give me a couple of days to talk to her. I don't want to delay things longer than I already have."

"Okay." Frost smiled. "Why don't we order lunch, and you can tell me about Hannah."

"I can do that."

FROST COULDN'T WIPE the big grin off his face. He didn't know what happened to Zane while he was gone, but he thanked his lucky stars that the man came back with his mind and heart, willing to accept their mating.

They were walking hand in hand at the mall, window shopping. Frost didn't know if it was his joyous mood, but everything seemed to be brighter and crisper, from the Christmas lights on the wreaths and garlands to the

Christmas tree and the music blasting in the air. He wasn't even bothered that the place was crowded with shoppers. And it might have his imagination but he thought everyone else was smiling along with him.

What made him shake his head a little was the long line to meet Santa Claus. Frost knew the man sitting in the high wingback chair wasn't his uncle Nick, but an imposter. However, it didn't stop Nick from sending out his secret elves to find out what kids and adults wanted for Christmas. The elf on the shelf wasn't just a wooden figure that liked to trick people. They were agents sent to watch who's been bad or good and report back to headquarters in Wynter Spell.

"Are you going to bring Hannah to meet Santa Claus?"

Zane shook his head.

"Why not? Don't tell me she doesn't believe in Santa Claus?"

"You hit the nail on the head," he responded.

"You have to be joking," Frost said in surprise.

"With all the magic in the world and the fact that she's part witch and werewolf, she doesn't think he's real."

Frost stared at Zane. "That's impossible. Every kid believes in Santa."

"Well, mine doesn't. She knows I'm the one that puts the presents under the tree every year."

"He is real, and I can prove it to her."

Zane lightly gripped his shoulder and pulled him close, kissing him on the forehead. "You don't have to do that. Hannah is a very strong-minded person—just like her mother."

Frost heard his words, but his mind was focused on the tingling on his forehead from Zane's kiss. He'd received many of them today at lunch, and his body was still warm all over.

"Come on, let's continue walking around. I'm not ready to end our date yet."

Frost nodded. As they passed by Santa Claus, he stopped when he recognized Perry, an elf from Wynter Spell, helping the imposter, and a plan formulated in his mind. Perry looked in his direction and nodded in recognition, not moving toward him. "Do you know what Hannah wants for Christmas?"

"A dog, but I keep telling her no. Having a pet is an enormous responsibility. But other than that, she's been begging me for some new game."

Oh, that is perfect, Frost thought. He looked at Perry, sending him a wink. Frost knew Perry would seek him out later, and that was when he would make things happen.

"I HAD A GOOD TIME TODAY." They were walking back to Frost's office. It was snowing, but neither seemed to mind.

"I did, too. I can't wait for us to do this more often," Frost said.

"Speaking of spending more time together, be my date for my company party?"

"You think that's a good idea?"

"I do." Zane knew their date had to end, but he wanted to be with Frost more and more. Their mating bond was almost stretched to the limits because of him, and he did not want his little fae to feel rejected anymore.

"Why?"

"There are many ways to answer that question, but I will give you three. One, you're my mate. Two..."

"Stop," Frost said. "Say that again."

Zane quirked a brow. "What, two?"

"No, the other part."

"I'm not sure what you're talking about." Zane bit his lips to stop himself from laughing when Frost's cheeks puffed up as he pouted. It was cute and childish, but Zane enjoyed seeing this side of the man. However, he knew the longer he pretended not to know what the fae was talking about, the angrier he might become. Their bonding was on a tightrope as it was already. He circled an arm around Frost's waist, pulling the shorter man close to him, lightly grasping his chin and raising his gaze to his. "You are my mate, Frostland Winterbourne, and at the stroke of midnight, you're the only one I want to be kissing. From now on, we will be tied together."

He gazed heatedly at his mate and became increasingly jealous of the snowflake that fell on his lips. Slowly, he lowered his head and pressed their lips together, and despite the cold air, Zane was warm from head to toe. His heart banged against his chest as if threatening to burst when Frost wrapped his arms around his neck and pulled him close. Their kiss deepened, and Zane felt their bond grow stronger, confirming his decision to give love another chance.

FROST MOANED, locking his arms around Zane's neck, threading his fingers through the man's dark, soft hair. He whimpered, opening himself up entirely to the other man when his large tongue swept into his mouth, and he felt as if he were being devoured whole. Frost had been kissed before, but never like this. He wanted to strip the man completely bare, licking every inch of his body, then letting Zane fuck him until he couldn't walk.

However, he had enough sense to remember that they were standing outside, which meant getting naked wouldn't be a good idea. But it didn't stop him from enjoying the taste and feel of Zane. It was just as he had imagined—all-consuming and breathtaking. With just one kiss, Frost felt possessed and did not want to be released.

Their mouths and tongues entwined, teasing and flirting with each other as their bodies melded together. Frost's heart beat to a rhythm of lust and want, making his chest grow tight as he grew increasingly breathless. Frost wasn't sure how long they were kissing, but he didn't want to stop. Unfortunately, Zane slowly separated their mouths, pressing their foreheads together. Their panting breaths echoed in his ear.

"So, will you be my date?" Zane whispered.

Frost opened his eyes, and their gaze connected. "Okay."

"Good." Zane tightened his arms around his waist and captured his mouth once more, taking away all of his senses.

CHAPTER EIGHT

Zane hummed, walking into his home. He was still soaring high from his date with Frost. He hung up his coat and paused when he didn't see Hannah come to greet him, since they hadn't seen each other for days. It was still early and nowhere close to her bedtime.

While he was away, he had asked Megan to watch his daughter. Usually, he'd have his two best friends take care of Hannah whenever he had to go out of town, but they had gone away for a few days. Just as he was about to search for the two of them, he heard laughter coming from the kitchen and headed that way. He paused at the doorway when he saw Megan and Hannah busy making cookies. He didn't alert them to his presence and watched them for a few minutes. He was happy to see Hannah not stuck to one of her game consoles.

"Be careful, they are still a little warm," Megan said gently.

"Okay," Hannah said, moving the cookies from the rack to the tray. "Do you think Daddy will like them?"

"Of course he will. You made them," Megan answered,

smiling brightly. "Hannah, did you have fun with me these past days?"

"I sure did; you were fun."

"Do you think I'd make a good mommy?"

Zane's brows furrowed, wondering where Megan was going with that question.

"Sure," Hannah answered.

Megan sat down beside her, brushing a lock of hair behind her ear. "Would you like for me to be your mommy? We could go shopping like we did this week or bake, and we had so much fun putting up the Christmas decorations. We could do so many other things if I were your mom, don't you think?"

Zane didn't like hearing the conversation, but he wanted to hear Hannah's response.

"Maybe," Hannah softly responded. "But I don't think it's a good idea."

"Why not?"

"Daddy said he doesn't want to be with anyone other than my mommy."

"Oh," Megan said. "But she's n..."

Guessing what Megan was about to say, Zane made his presence known. "What is that delicious scent?"

They both looked over their shoulders, and Hannah smiled happily, jumped off the chair, and ran over to him. He scooped her up, lavishing her with hugs and kisses, and soon the kitchen was filled with her laughter.

"I missed you, my sweet baby," Hannah said.

"I missed you too, Daddy. Guess what?"

"What?"

"Megan and I made cookies."

"Really?" Zane said in shock and turned his gaze to Megan, giving her a serious look versus the doting one he had for Hannah. She was smiling just as happily as Hannah, but as if noticing something was wrong, the smile on her face instantly slipped into a frown.

Zane looked at Hannah. "Hey, Han, why don't you go change your clothes? I want to take you to dinner."

"Can Megan come with us?" she asked.

"Not tonight. I think Megan mentioned she had something to do. Isn't that right?" he said, looking over to Megan who seemed to get his meaning.

"Your daddy is right. I promised a couple of friends I'd meet them for dinner. You guys go on without me. Maybe next time."

Hannah's disappointment showed on her face, but she instantly perked up when he tweaked her nose. "I'll take you wherever you want to go."

"Really?" she asked excitedly.

"Yes." Putting her down, he ruffled her hair. "Go on."

Hannah nodded, waved bye to Megan, and then ran out of the kitchen. Once Zane made sure she was gone, he turned to Megan.

"Thank you for watching Hannah for me while I went out of the country. You've been a big help to me." He pulled out his cellphone and electronically sent her some money to cover any expenses for the week. "I don't think I'll be needing your help anymore."

"You heard my conversation with Hannah, didn't you?"

"I did."

"Zane, I didn't..."

"If I've ever given you the impression that I'm looking for more than just friendship, I'm sorry," he said, cutting her off. He'd never led her on or given her any indication that he was attracted to her. "I'm grateful for everything you've done for Hannah and me. But..."

"I'm not your type," she finished for him.

Zane didn't respond. There was nothing he could say. Zane didn't have a type, he never had. To him, love and chemistry were all that mattered. He had found it with Arizona, and now, with Frost in his life, he had a second chance to experience it again.

"I did everything for you to notice how much I wanted to be with you. I kept telling myself you needed time, but I can see you'll never open your heart." Tears welled in her eyes. "I feel like a fool."

"You shouldn't. You will find someone who will love you."

"But I want you," she cried. "You're the only man I can see myself with." She stepped forward and went to grab his face, but Zane moved back quickly.

"I think you should go," he said, seeing her embarrassment; however, it was not enough for her to leave immediately.

"I should get my things and say bye to Hannah."

"No," Zane said. "I'll have them sent to your house."

She nodded and ran out of the kitchen. Zane watched her leave, hoping the fates would send her someone who would love her for life. Taking a deep breath, he pulled out his cellphone and called Frost.

"Miss me already?" Frost asked, bringing a smile to Zane's face.

I just wanted to hear your voice, Zane thought, but instead, he said, "What are you doing tonight?"

"I have a family," Frost said. "With Christmas coming, we get pretty busy in my family. But I doubt you called me to ask me that. What's up?"

"Daddy, I'm ready," Hannah shouted from the other room.

"Hey, I gotta go. I'll call you later."

"I'll wait up for your call," Frost told him.

"Okay."

They hung up, Zane pocketed his phone, and hummed as he met Hannah for their dinner date.

FROST HUNG UP THE PHONE, smiling. He hadn't expected Zane's call, but he was thrilled to hear the man's voice.

"What are you so happy about?" Nyx asked.

"Zane just called me," Frost told him.

"Oh. So when are you going to tell the parents that you've found your mate?"

Frost groaned. "Do I have to tell them?"

"Do you think you can hide your mate from them for long?"

Frost knew it was a silly endeavor, but he wanted to savor the sweet moments with Zane before he involved his parents. They weren't pushy, but they were the kind of parents that wanted grandkids right away. Although he loved and wanted kids, he wasn't ready to have his own. He saw what happened to his sister after she found her mate. Every time his parents saw her they'd ask for grandkids. The only thing that might save Frost from the grandkids inquisition was the fact that Zane had a daughter.

Frost sat up abruptly and looked at his brother. "He wants me to meet his daughter."

"How do you feel about that?"

"I'm fine with it. I think it's better to create a bond with her before Zane and I have kids. I don't want her to feel left out."

Nyx peered at Frost for a few minutes before he spoke. "Your thoughts have become more mature, little brother."

"What's that supposed to mean?"

"You're thinking of someone else's feelings other than your own." Nyx smiled and stood. "Keep it up, little brother. Come on, let's go, the parents are waiting for us."

"You make it sound as if I've never considered others' feelings," Frost grumbled, then looked at his brother's disappearing back. He'd never denied that he was a selfish person, but he'd never hurt someone just to get what he wanted. Manipulate them, sure, but that was as far as he went. After all, he wanted to stay on his uncle Nick's nice list.

ZANE TRAILED a finger along his lips. He couldn't stop smiling as he recalled the kiss he and Frost shared earlier that day. They met up for lunch every day that week and, before departing, shared heated kisses. There were so many times he wanted to bring the man home and fuck him until he couldn't walk but held back because he needed to talk to Hannah first, which was something he had been putting off.

They were getting comfortable around each other as the bond deepened between them. They'd talked about everything, like when to start a family.

"I want to wait a little while before we think about having kids," Frost said one day at lunch.

"Why?"

"Hannah and I need to develop our own bond, and we need to grow as a family before we introduce more children."

Hearing Frost's explanation, Zane had to agree. After Frost met Hannah, he would be introduced to Frost's family. He was ready for the new phase in their mating and couldn't wait to make love to the fae and have him fall asleep in his arms. Looking at the time, he noted that it was still early, and Zane picked up his phone to give Frost a quick call, but stopped when his office door opened and the prettiest face with a head full of curly hair appeared.

"Daddy, are you busy?"

Zane smiled, setting his phone down. "When it comes to you, I'm never busy."

Hannah walked over and jumped on his lap. It was then he noticed she had a sheet of paper in her hand. "What do you have here?"

"My Christmas list," she replied sweetly.

"Oh." Zane took the paper and read over the list. Like every year, she didn't ask for much, and a dog was at the top of the list, followed by a couple of popular toys and a new gaming system, since she was an avid gamer even at a young age. Zane had remembered teaching Hannah how to play one game when she was around five, and she took to it like a fish to water.

Hannah was one of the reasons his company invested heavily in gaming and domestic and international competition. He didn't know what her future would hold but had no problem supporting the things she enjoyed doing. Not only that, but she was one of his company's beta testers for the games related to her age group.

"Are you sure you don't want to send this list off to the North Pole for Santa Claus?" he asked, looking down at her.

Zane chuckled when she sighed exaggeratedly. "Daddy, you're too old to believe in fairy tales."

"Aren't you the one who suggested the fairy-tale-themed party for my office?"

"Yes, but that's because I thought it was a good idea." She shrugged her little shoulders. "That's all."

"I think you do believe in fairy tales and are just pretending," Zane joked. "That's why I think you're kidding me when you say you don't think Santa Claus is real."

"He's not," she said, crossing her arms over her chest and giving him a stubborn look that reminded him so much of Arizona.

"How are you so sure?"

"Because he never gave me what I asked for," she said sadly.

That caught Zane's attention. *What could she have asked Santa for?* He put the paper down, lifting her up and setting her on his desk. "What did you ask Santa for, my sweet one?"

She shook her head, refusing to say.

"Come on, baby, tell me."

"If...if I tell you, you'll be sad."

Zane smiled and caressed her cheeks. "Nothing you say will make me sad."

She stared at him for a few seconds, then blurted out. "I asked him for a new mommy." Hannah jumped in his arms. "I'm sorry, Daddy. I know how much you miss Mommy, and it's selfish of me to want a new mommy, but..."

Zane didn't let her finish. He held her close. "It's okay, and you're not being selfish. Wanting to have the love of two parents is perfectly fine. Hey, look at me." She shook her head, burrowing herself in his chest. Zane sighed. "Is that why you kept asking me what I thought of Megan?" She nodded, still not looking at him. "Why didn't you tell me, Hannah?"

At that question, she looked up at him, tears staining her face. "Because I heard you tell Uncle Seb that you will never find someone else to love, but I thought if Santa brought one to you, you might change your mind. And when you smiled at Megan, I thought you liked her."

Zane couldn't recall what conversation she could have overheard. He had said those words to every one of his friends until he was blue in the face, countless times over the years. He reached for some tissue and cleaned off her face.

"Do you remember what Daddy told you about mates?" Even though she was half witch, half werewolf, she hadn't shown any signs of carrying either of the genes, but he had never hidden anything about their history.

Hannah sniffled and nodded. "The gods will give us the perfect opportunity to meet the one we are supposed to love."

"Yes, but I didn't tell you that sometimes they also give us two."

Hannah gasped. "Two?"

"Yes." He smiled. "After your mommy died, I was sad and didn't want to accept it, so I made a promise never to fall in love again. But I've recently changed my mind. Do you understand what I'm saying?" Hannah shook her head, and Zane figured it would be better to say things plainly. "I know you like her, Han, but Megan is not my mate."

"It's okay, Daddy. She's very nice, but she's not your mate."

"But there is someone special I want you to meet. He is my mate."

Zane thought she would have smiled hearing that, but her lips turned down into a cute pout. "Baby, what's wrong?"

"You said they were special. Does that make them your new favorite?"

Zane laughed and pulled her into his arms, hugging her tightly. "You'll always be my number one priority."

"Promise?" she whispered.

"I do." He hated the sadness he heard in her tone. Zane sometimes forgot that Hannah was still a child, even though she might act far older than her age. "No matter who comes into our lives."

"Okay."

They sat like that until Hannah fell asleep. He didn't talk any more about her meeting Frost. After putting her in bed, Zane leaned against the headboard, gazing down at her as he tried to think of a way for her and Frost to meet and not let Hannah feel upset about the whole thing. When nothing came to him, Zane kissed Hannah good night and went to bed. He had to believe that he would figure things out soon.

FROST KNOCKED on the door to Lisa and Mark's home and was instantly greeted by Lisa, who had an adorable little girl that he recognized standing next to her.

Hannah Moon-Blood, why is she here?

Frost couldn't take his eyes off Hannah. He knew she resembled Arizona, but there were also parts of Zane that he recognized. Like the curious way she was staring at him.

"Frost, what are you doing here? Is something wrong?" Lisa asked.

"There are a couple of things I wanted to go over with you since your wedding is coming up," he said, taking his eyes off Hannah and holding up his portfolio. "Usually, I'd have you come to my office, but since I was in the neighborhood, I figured I might as well stop by. If you're not available, I can schedule a meeting."

"Nah, come on in," Lisa said.

"Cool, thanks."

"It's not a problem." She smiled and stepped aside, giving him room to enter the house. "I'm sorry, Hannah. I know your uncle and I promised to take you to the movies, but we need to talk with Mr. Winterbourne."

"It's okay, Auntie Lisa. We can go later." Hannah smiled sweetly.

"Oh, how rude of me. Frost, this is my niece, Hannah Blood-Moon," Lisa said, cupping her cheek. "Hannah, this is our friend and our wedding planner, Frost."

"Hello, it's nice to meet you, Mister Frost," Hannah said sweetly.

"Hannah, that's a pretty name for a princess," Frost said and was pleased when the girl smiled. Her light brown complexion and dark curly hair complemented her bright hazel eyes. "I'm not a princess." She giggled.

"Oh, I beg to differ." He waved a hand over her hair, mumbling a simple spell. When he removed his hand, an ice crown was nestled in her mound of curls.

"Wow," Lisa said in awe. "Are you sure you're in the right profession?"

"What do you mean?" Although it was frowned upon for his kind to do magic in front of humans, Frost had never adhered to that rule. He thought as long as he didn't go over the top, the supernatural council wouldn't come knocking at his front door.

"Don't get me wrong, you're an awesome event planner, but your magical skills are amazing," Lisa gushed. "You should take this act on the road."

Frost and Hannah looked at each other, and he winked

at her as if sending her a secret message, making her giggle. "Want to look in the mirror?" he asked, avoiding Lisa's comment.

Hannah eagerly nodded.

"Come on." He guided her to the hallway mirror and watched her admire herself.

Hannah reached up and touched the tiara. "It's cold like ice."

"It will harden then turn into crystal, so be careful not to break it."

"Okay," she said, looking back at herself in the mirror.

"She's adorable," Frost said.

"Hannah's dad and Mark are good friends. She's Mark's goddaughter. We're watching her for a day."

"Oh," Frost said. *So that answers a couple of questions, like how Zane might have found my business. Lisa and Mark must have recommended him.*

"I can't believe you made something like that. If I didn't know any better, I'd start believing you have real magical powers," Lisa joked.

Frost chuckled, not giving anything away. "Is there somewhere we can talk? I promise it won't be long."

"Yeah, come on," she said to him. "Hannah, I'll be back."

"Okay, Auntie Lisa."

CHAPTER NINE

"Frost, I can't thank you enough," Lisa praised as she walked him back to the front door. "You took so much pressure off me and Mark."

Frost smiled. "It's what you're paying me the big bucks for. Anyway, I'll see you in a few days. Until then, try and relax."

"Easier said than done," Lisa said, opening the door. Frost was about to walk out but stepped back in surprise when he saw Zane with his hand seeming about to knock on the door. They stared at each other in shock.

"Zane, what are you doing here?" Lisa asked instead of Frost. "I thought Hannah was spending the night."

Zane cleared his throat, held up a stuffed toy rabbit, and spoke, not taking his eyes off Frost. "Hannah forgot to pack her rabbit. I know she acts older than her age, but she doesn't like sleeping without it."

"Oh." Lisa chuckled and winked. "We all have our secrets."

"I didn't think I'd see you today," Zane commented.

"Yeah, I had some wedding things to discuss with Lisa."

"Ah, so you're the one organizing their wedding. I should have known," Zane said. "Lisa couldn't stop bragging about their wedding planner."

"Isn't that how you ended up in my office?" he asked, not understanding why Zane would say that.

Zane shook his head. "I was walking down your street after a meeting and saw your sign, and before I could think about what was happening, I made an appointment."

"Wait, you two know each other?" Lisa questioned, looking between them.

Zane stepped closer to Frost and pulled him into a one-arm hug. "We're dating."

Lisa screamed in joy, then rushed to them, giving them an excited hug. "Oh my gods! This is awesome. Do you know how long Mark and I have been trying to get Zane to start dating? He's been alone for far too long."

"What the hell is all the screaming?" Mark came rushing into the room, followed by Hannah, whose tiara had now crystallized.

"Zane and Frost are dating," Lisa shouted, rushing over to her fiance.

"Daddy," Hannah yelled happily, running over to her father, who bent down and scooped her up. "Are you taking me home?"

"Hey, baby." Zane kissed her on the cheek. "I thought you wanted to spend the night with Uncle Mark and Auntie Lisa?"

"Not anymore." She pouted. "He's mean."

"Hey, what did you do to my kid?" Zane growled, but Frost knew there was no bite to his tone.

"She's just a sore loser." Mark shrugged.

"She's a kid; you're supposed to let her win," his fiancee said, smacking him on the back of his head.

"How else is she supposed to learn if we let her win at everything," Mark defended then looked at Zane. "Anyway, that's not the important issue. When were you going to tell us you stepped from under the dark clouds and stepped into the light of love?"

Zane's arms tightened around Frost, making him turn his gaze to his mate. "Well, I'm telling you now. Frost and I are dating...no, Frost and I are getting married."

"What?" Mark and Lisa said in shock.

Zane winked, and just like that, Frost understood. They didn't know he was a werewolf and knew nothing about mates, so it was the best way to explain things.

"Wait, how long have you two been dating?" Mark asked.

"Long enough to know he's the one for me."

Mark and Zane stared at each other, and Frost could feel some tension creeping into the room; before it could spike, Mark smiled and reached out to hug his friend.

"Good. Be happy, my friend," Mark said, clapping Zane on his back. He turned to Frost. "Don't break his heart."

"You don't have to worry about that because it will never happen."

Zane chuckled and kissed him on the forehead.

A TIGHTENING on his neck had him looking at Hannah, and it was then he noticed the sparkling tiara in her hair. It didn't look like something that was bought in any store. He touched it and smiled, feeling the magic radiating from it, and guessed it was Frost's doing. Truthfully, he wanted Hannah to be the first person to meet Frost over his friends, but the fates must have gotten tired of waiting on them to get their foot out of their asses.

I guess now is as good a time as any. "Hey, guys, I think I'm going to take Hannah home," Zane said, using his eyes to convey his meaning to his friends.

"It's all good," Mark said. "Go do your thing."

"Thanks." Zane looked at Frost. "Mind joining me and this beautiful princess for dinner?"

"Sure."

"Come on." Zane was guiding them to the door when Frost stopped them. "What's up?"

"Hannah's bags. Where are they? How about her coat?"

"Oh, it's all right. She has a room and stuff here." Just as he spoke, Mark brought over Hannah's coat, and Frost helped her put it on.

"Okay, all set, let's go," Frost said.

"Where's your car?" Zane asked when they got outside. It had started snowing during the short time he was inside.

"I didn't drive. I teleported here."

"Do you always use your magic so freely? What if you were seen?"

"Please don't nag, I get it enough from my brother, Nyx."

"I..."

"Introduce me properly to your daughter," Frost smiled, stopping any lecture Zane was ready to give.

"I see what you're trying to do, and this once I'll let it go. But we'll discuss things in more detail later."

"Yes, dear." Frost chuckled, and Zane couldn't help but follow.

He wanted to pull the fae to him and kiss him until his mouth was bruised and red. Zane licked his lips at how tempted he was to take more but held back. He couldn't deny that it was getting harder to resist the man's charms. He was dying to fuck the man, driving the fae out of his mind, when just a few weeks ago he was against being with anyone.

Zane knew it was the pull of the bond, but in order for him to have those thoughts, it also meant that he wanted it just as well. But all of that had to wait. Zane looked at Hannah, who was still in his arms. Soft snowflakes dusted her face, and the crystal tiara sitting on top of her head seemed more like a halo thanks to the light coming from the light above the door.

"Baby girl, do you remember when I told you I met someone special to me?" Hannah nodded. "Well, this is my friend...no, this is my mate, Frost, and I would love for you two to get to know each other."

Hannah leaned closed and whispered in his ear, "Daddy, put me down, please."

Zane furrowed his brows but did as she asked. He watched as she stood in front of Frost and looked at him, unafraid. "Do you really like my Daddy?"

Frost smiled and kneeled, taking her hand. "Yes, I do."

"I don't want another mommy," Hannah said, shocking Zane, and he thought Frost would have been offended.

"Whew, that's good to hear, because I don't want to be your mommy. I want to be your friend as we get to know each other. We can change what we call each other later." He raised his gaze to Zane then back to Hannah. "All I ask is that you give me a chance."

Hannah was silent for a few minutes. "Okay. I can do that."

"Thank you, Hannah. Can I hug you?"

Hannah nodded, and Frost pulled her into his arms. A smile crossed Zane's lips; he couldn't help but pull out his cellphone and take a picture, capturing the moment. Zane watched the two for a few minutes more, and he could feel the bond extending not only between him and Frost but to Hannah as well. He could also feel the gap in his heart slowly closing.

After a while, Hannah and Frost separated, and they smiled at each other.

"Thank you for my tiara," Hannah said. "I love it."

"I'm glad. I'll make you a bracelet and earrings to match," Frost told her.

"Really?" Hannah said excitedly. "Can I ask you a question?"

"Of course."

She motioned for Frost to move closer. "Are you an elf?" she whispered.

Frost chuckled and shook his head. "No, I'm a fae, but I am related to a few elves you will meet soon. You see, they work for an exceptional guy who I call Uncle Nick, but some refer to him as—" Frost stopped and bit his lips. "Better yet, I'll introduce him to you on Christmas Eve. After all, now that we're family, you'll be going to Wynter Spell with me."

"Wynter Spell?" Zane and Hannah said together.

Frost stood. "Yes, it's where I'm from.

Zane went to ask more questions, but Frost stopped him. "Let's not talk anymore out here. We're making Mark and Lisa worry." He pointed to the house, and it was then that Zane noticed his friends were standing at the window watching them. He waved at them, and they hurriedly closed the curtains.

"You're right. Let's go have dinner and talk." He guided Frost and Hannah toward his car. As they walked, they discussed what they wanted to eat. It was so comforting, and it made the moment feel as if they were a true family.

ZANE WALKED QUIETLY, closed Hannah's bedroom door, and then slowly took the stairs down to the sitting room where Frost was waiting. They'd had a great night or Zane had thought so. Since it wasn't a school night, instead of going to a restaurant, they went miniature golfing, where Hannah got to eat all the junk food she wanted.

For the first half of the night, Hannah stayed by his side, but as the night wore on, she clung to Frost as if he was her best friend. Although it was their first time meeting, Zane had hoped things would turn out okay. They were having so much fun they never got to hear more about Wynter Spell from Frost. Zane had never heard of the place.

Could it be another magical town? There's so much about our world I don't know. And who do the elves work for?

When he got to the sitting room he noticed that Frost was not there. His home wasn't huge, but it also wasn't small. The house had three stories, with four bedrooms, two of which were master suites. He'd transformed the remaining bedrooms into a home office he'd shared with Arizona, a playroom for Hannah, and a movie and game room. After Arizona died Zane had thought of selling the three-story home but changed his mind. He remembered how she loved the spacious layout.

Because Arizona had loved to cook, Zane had redesigned the kitchen, equipping it with state-of-the-art appliances and ample counter space, with an island that was the center of the room, where they often entertained with their friends, forgoing the dining room. So it didn't surprise Zane when he found Frost preparing tea. He leaned against the door and watched as his mate made himself at home.

I once shared this home with Arizona, but will Frost want to live here? If he doesn't, I have no problems moving, but I have to think of Hannah.

Zane recalled Hannah and Frost ganging up on him to win the game. They really got along in only a couple of hours.

"Did you have fun tonight?" Zane asked.

"I did," Frost said, turning around. "I like Hannah, and I hope she likes me too."

"Are you kidding me?" Zane said. "She likes you. It took her a while to warm up to Megan."

"Megan? Who's Megan?"

Zane bit his tongue to hold back his laughter; he didn't miss the jealousy in Frost's voice.

"Megan...Megan..." Zane tapped his chin, trying to stall, only to feel a cold and sharp point piercing his chin.

"Don't play with me, wolf man." Zane was a little surprised the fae had moved so fast. However, he wasn't afraid, knowing the man wouldn't and couldn't hurt him. "Do I need to remind you exactly who you belong to?" He quirked a brow. "Now, do you want to answer my question?"

Zane smirked, grabbed Frost's fingers, which were cold like ice, and brought them to his lips, kissing the icicles.

"Megan is my next-door neighbor who has looked after Hannah for me on many occasions."

"Are you attracted to Megan?"

"No," Zane answered honestly and wrapped his arms around Frost's waist. "So, am I safe?"

"More than safe, you're lucky." Frost stepped out of his arms and leaned against the island. "In fact, I have to make a confession."

"Really, what's that?" Zane quirked a brow and walked closer to him, but they didn't touch. He stared intensely into his bright blue eyes, feeling trapped but not scared.

"I knew about Hannah and your wife. Before you told me."

Zane took a step back, feeling somewhat uncomfortable. "What? Explain what you mean by that."

"My brother ran an investigation on you."

"When?" Zane growled, feeling his anger rise.

"The day we met in my office, I went to see my brother and got pretty drunk. I told him you rejected me and might have begged him to ruin your company. Normally, my brother would ignore my drunken rants, but I found out that he paid attention this time. I'm not sure what he did, but I told him to seek you out and apologize."

"What about you? Don't you think you owe me one as well?" His quickly rising anger slowly calmed down as he focused on Frost's words.

Zane wanted to be angry. Hell, he should've been fuming, but his company's profits seemed to skyrocket overnight, and he had more people banging down his door to invest in the new game they were developing. Zane guessed he could attribute that to Frost's brother for righting his wrong. He could also admit that what happened was partly his fault.

"You're right." Frost closed the gap between them, pressing his body flush against Zane's, resting his hands on his chest as he slightly tilted his head, showing his neck, a sure sign of submission, but it was the look in his eyes that caught Zane's interest. "How do you want me to say I'm sorry?"

Zane licked his lips, feeling his chest tighten with the need to bite and mark the spotless neck. "You're good at distracting me from my anger."

"Is that what you think I'm doing?"

Zane circled his waist with one hand and cupped the back of his head with the other. "Yes, but right now, I don't care." Zane lowered his head and pressed their lips together. A soft moan escaped Frost's mouth the second they touched. Frost wrapped a hand around Zane's neck. The fae's lips felt like heaven against his, soft and firm. Their kiss was a slow, sensual dance, each movement designed to tease and tantalize. Clearly, they had no intentions of rushing things; their desire for each other only grew stronger with each passing moment.

CHAPTER TEN

Zane's tongue devoured Frost's mouth with the hunger of the wolf; he was igniting the fire between them. He savored every whimper and moan that escaped Frost's lips. He moved his hand down and slipped them into the back of Frost's pants, kneading and groping his meaty ass possessively without breaking their kiss.

Zane's erection pressed uncomfortably against his zipper. Frost's hand moved between them and started unbuttoning Zane's pants. He released Frost's ass and helped his mate push both their trousers and underwear below their asses. They both hissed when their cocks sprang out, and the heads of their erection brushed against each other.

They pressed flush against each other, grinding and swirling their hips. Their lips separated in the desire for breath, and Frost buried his face in Zane's chest. The scent of peaches and vanilla mixed with mint and pine wafted around them, driving Zane mad with need.

"Zane, more," Frost moaned. "I need more."

Zane opened his eyes and came in contact with Frost's

unblemished neck. He felt his canines elongate with the need to bite and mark his mate. Leaning down, he nuzzled Frost's neck as his scent grew more intense. Zane grazed his sharp teeth along his flesh as their hips moved faster. Frost's nails dug into his skin, almost ripping his shirt, but Zane didn't care. He could feel his orgasm building. His mind grew hazy and his heart thundered in his chest.

It had been so long since he'd had a lover, so long since he sank his canines into supple flesh, tasting their blood and feeling their magical bond grow between them. He wanted and needed to feel Frost come undone against him.

"Bite me," he heard Frost say. "Make me yours."

Are you sure? Zane wanted to ask, but his mouth was somehow filled with saliva as he was sucking and tasting his mate's sweet skin before he bit down hard but did not break the flesh. Even with that action he could feel the threads of their bond surrounding them but was unable to see it.

"Zane, I'm gonna..." Frost moaned, unable to get the words out as Zane felt his mate cumming between them. It didn't take Zane long to follow right behind him. Their hips slowed but did not stop moving as they both rode out their orgasm, feeling the sweet waves pass through them.

Fuck, that felt good.

"WHY DIDN'T YOU BITE ME?" Frost asked.

They were standing in the same spot in a slight state of undress, holding each other for Grand-Odin knew how long. Frost had thought and hoped Zane would bite him, marking him so they could complete the mating bond.

Zane gently grabbed the back of Frost's neck, lifting his

head. "Sexy as it is, I don't want the first time I'm balls deep inside of you to be in my kitchen."

"Then take me somewhere private," Frost suggested.

"I want to make love to you so bad, but..."

"Not tonight," Frost finished for him. Zane nodded, not sure he could explain what he was thinking or feeling. Despite what they just did, Zane wanted the perfect mood.

"Okay," Frost said. "Then how about we do something else?"

"Like what?"

Frost cupped his cheeks. "How about we go for a run?"

"As much as I would love to, I can't leave Hannah alone."

"I know, and she won't be alone." Frost smiled. "While you were putting Hannah to bed, I placed a magical barrier around the house."

Zane went to speak, but Frost stopped him.

"Before you say that's not enough, the tiara she refuses to take off, along with the earrings and bracelet, has a magical tracking charm. Where she goes, I'll know." He cupped Zane's cheek and touched his head, pressing their foreheads together. He shivered when he felt a new bond between him and Hannah. "I know you have your bond with her. This is just a bonus."

Zane nodded, then raised his head. "This is all good, but I won't leave her alone."

"And she won't be. Ellie will watch her."

"Ellie? What or who is an Ellie?" Zane asked, completely confused.

"That would be me, mate of Frostland Winterbourne."

Zane turned at the soft voice and blinked a few times, seeing a female elf dressed in a red jumpsuit, a broad white collar, and a matching red-and-white Santa hat. Her cheeks were rosy, and her bright green eyes lit her face.

An elf. How did an elf get in my house, and I did not know about it?

"Zane, get dressed. We don't want Ellie to see more than she should," Frost said as he righted his clothes and helped Zane with his.

"Hello, Ellie. I haven't seen you in a while," Frost said, walking over to the elf.

"You've blown my cover, young Frostland," Ellie replied, looking over Frost's shoulder. "But I understand."

Frost looked at Zane, smiling. "Zane, I'd like for you to meet Scout Ellie Evergreen. Your very own elf on the shelf and a helper to my uncle Nick, who everyone calls Santa Claus."

"Get the fuck out of here," he said in shock. Zane looked between them and felt like his world had just expanded.

FROST CHUCKLED, looking at Zane's shocked expression, and then he turned back to Ellie. "Do you mind watching Hannah for us? We're going for a little run."

"Certainly." Ellie giggled.

"Wait...wait..." Zane said. "What do you mean by all of that? And how are you sure you can trust her? No offense," he said, looking at Ellie.

"None taken," Ellie said.

Frost understood Zane's apprehension about leaving his daughter with a stranger. But truthfully, Ellie was far from being one. An elf didn't just show up on the holidays; they popped in throughout the year, watching to see who was being good or bad and causing a little mischief occasionally.

"Zane, you don't need to worry. Elli's no stranger to your home."

"What do you mean by that?" Zane said tersely.

"I was assigned to your home a few years ago because..."

"Ellie, stop," Frost said. "I'll explain things to him."

"But you don't know everything," Ellie said.

"No, but I can guess. I don't want to get you into any more trouble."

"I'm not the first scout to be noticed, Frostland. How do you think the stories about Nick got started?" She smiled.

"So true." Frost looked at Zane, grabbed his hand, and disappeared before the werewolf could say anything. In seconds, they appeared in the nearest wooded area.

"What the fuck, Frost," Zane growled. "Warn me the next time you do that shit. It felt like my entire body was being torn apart. Worse than my first shift."

"I'm sorry, babe, but I'm really in the mood for a run, and if we had stayed there any longer, you'd have asked a bunch of unnecessary questions."

"Hey, I just left my daughter with someone I don't even know, so excuse the fuck out of me if I want to question them," Zane yelled.

"You're right. But like I keep saying, you have nothing to worry about. And I said I would explain, but let's do it after our run."

"No," Zane said sternly. "Talk to me now."

"Fuck, you're tenacious. Okay, have you heard of a town called Valleywood?"

"Yes, what about it?"

"Well, other than Valleywood, there are a few more magical towns. They are hidden all over the world. Some even refer to them as hidden realms. Wynter Spell is one of those hidden towns where Bronwyn and I came from. It is also where Nick Boroson and his helpers live."

Frost explained things about his uncle Nick, how most of the family worked at the workshop, and the helpers' jobs, or rather the ones he could talk about that did not break confidentiality. Zane listened with rapt interest, forgetting they were standing in the middle of the forest in freezing weather.

"You know, if I were human and you told me about Santa Claus and all that stuff, I'd think you lost all your marbles, right?" he said, much calmer.

Frost chuckled. Of course, he knew what it sounded like. Even some of their own kind didn't even believe in the existence of gods. So it was completely understandable that humans didn't believe in a jolly old man who only showed up once a year, leaving presents under their Christmas tree.

"So that's how Ellie fits into all of this?"

"Yes. Have you ever noticed her before?"

Zane was quiet for a few minutes. "I don't remember." Zane leaned against a tree trunk. "I guess it was the first Christmas after Arizona died. I found the stuffed elf among the Christmas things she kept in the attic. Truthfully, it's not my favorite holiday, but Arizona loved this time of year. So I usually left all the holiday decorating to her, and I just assumed she bought it, thought nothing of it, and placed it on the shelf."

"Scouts aren't sold in stores. It means Ellie was assigned to your home."

"Fuck, the more I learn about our world, the more confused I get. It's why I've never tied myself down to a sect or a pack. Even though I have a drop of lykosian blood, I doubt the sect would accept me."

"But that's where you're wrong. Duncan Pryde is not that kind of man."

"How do you know?" Zane said, frowning.

"I've coordinated events for him, and his sect is filled with all kinds of shifters. Even a dracomen."

Zane's eyes widened as he heard that. He knew after the great war, quite a few sects went into hiding, including the dracomens. "Maybe I should seek out Duncan Pryde after all."

"But you do have a pack. You have Hannah and now me. And it will only get bigger once you meet my family and when we have children."

"I like the sound of that."

"Good. Now let's go for a run." *Since someone left me pent up.* He unbuttoned his shirt, took it off, and threw it to the ground. He sighed when the cold air touched his heated skin, cooling him down a bit. He was about to shift, releasing his wings and removing the magical glamor he wore daily, but paused when Zane spoke.

"I can't shake the feeling you're not telling me everything."

"I'm not," Frost told him the truth. "Babe, if I told you everything, your head would explode." He moved over to Zane and cupped his cheeks. "I want you to know everything about my magical, complicated, and sometimes confusing family. But truthfully, even I don't know everything about them. So for now, take what you know and lock it away, and let's enjoy what's left of this gorgeous night."

Because, unlike Nyx, Ellie can't keep a secret, and by the end of the week, my parents will be knocking on your front door.

Zane took a deep breath and nodded. "Okay." He smiled. "I like that, by the way."

"What?"

"When you call me babe."

"I'll call you anything you want. Now strip, mister; I've been dying to ride on your wolf's back."

Zane chuckled, shook his head, and unbuttoned his shirt, shrugging it off and standing shirtless in front of Frost, who had seen him partially naked countless times on the cover of a magazine. But what a glorious sight to see it in person.

"I take it you like what you see."

"Who wouldn't, when their crush is standing half-naked in front of them?"

"Crush?" Zane quirked a brow.

"A story for another time," Frost said, raising a hand and trailing a finger on the taller man's chest, circling a finger around his brown nipples that peaked at his touch. Frost leaned forward and brushed the tip of his tongue on the pebbled nub.

"I thought you wanted to go for a run." Zane cupped the back of his neck.

"I do, but who told you to be so alluring," Frost mumbled, covering the entire nipple and sucking it into his mouth. His intention was for them to go for a run, but how could he pass up a muscled, shirtless Zane? He had to tell himself not to go too far. He could tell Zane wasn't ready to jump into bed, but who said he couldn't taste the man just a little?

Just a little taste, that's all I want.

ZANE GRABBED FROST'S WAIST, pulling his hot body flush against his, hissing at the heat when they touched. He grasped a handful of Frost's hair, pulling his head back, and was surprised when the fae growled, baring his fangs at him, seeming annoyed at being interrupted.

"Simmer down, baby."

Although he said the words, Zane licked his lips, enjoying the sight of the fae's deep blue irises glowing in the moonlight as his proper form took over. Zane grazed his thumb against the points of Frost's ear, eliciting a shiver and a moan from his pretty lips. Then Zane noticed the faint markings on his face and neck, leading down to his arms. Zane couldn't tell if they were words or tribal tattoos, but he wanted to touch them.

Frost leaned forward and sniffed Zane's skin. "Mate," he moaned, digging his now-shifted claws into his chest and drawing blood. "Mine." The fae's words sounded slurred, as if he were drunk. He dragged his tongue from one nipple to the other, not forgetting to stop and lick up Zane's blood. He felt Frost's canines roughly scraping at his sensitive skin, ready to bite him. Zane pulled his head back, seeing his eyes drunk with lust.

"Why won't you let me taste?" Frost whined.

"Not yet," Zane said, kissing him quickly. "Shift for me, baby. Show me your pretty wings."

"Will you play with me if I do?" Frost said softly.

"Of course. It's one of the reasons we came out here."

Zane was enjoying the change in the fae, the sweet, submissive nature that came out, enchanting Zane even more.

"Okay," the fae responded compliantly.

Zane released his hair and stepped back, putting ample space between them. "Don't look away from me, my handsome mate."

"I won't."

Frost took off his shoes and socks, throwing them aside, and Zane followed suit, slipping off his pants and kicking off his shoes and socks. They were both standing naked in the snow, still not bothered by the cold. Zane was still aroused from their earlier play, even though he was the one who stopped it.

He had to admit the man's body was exquisite, especially in his partially shifted form and with magic swirling around him. Frost closed his eyes and took a deep breath, opening his arms, and expansive, transparent crystal wings flared behind him, shimmering in the moonlight, making the markings on his skin shine even brighter. Zane stepped forward to touch Frost's wings, but the fae opened his eyes and instantly took to the sky.

"Come play with me, my mate," he said, and Zane was surprised they had a mental link already, but he had no time to think on it, since Frost flew away, leaving behind trails of sparkling, shimmering magic dust. Frost giggled and flew away, leaving Zane no recourse but to shift and follow him. Zane shifted quickly and chased after him.

Zane wasn't sure what game they were playing, but it didn't matter to him. They were having fun. He enjoyed the wind running through his fur. They played for most of the night until Frost got tired. They settled under a large tree with Frost snuggling into his fur.

"So soft," Frost purred. *"I want to play again."*

"We will," Zane told him.

Frost was like a naughty imp, hiding from Zane several times and pretending to draw him close, only to run away and have Zane run after him again. He was like a child who wanted to play all night. Zane had to admit it was the most fun he'd had in a very long time.

They were relaxing, and Zane almost fell asleep but was startled when Frost sat up.

"The baby is in trouble," the fae said. Before Zane could say anything, they disappeared from the spot under the tree and reappeared in the living room. Frost shifted and ran up the stairs. Zane followed suit, but unlike Frost, he grabbed the blanket off the back of the couch, wrapping it around his waist, and ran up the stairs.

He got upstairs to Hannah's room just in time to see Frost helping Ellie off the floor, with blood coming down the side of her face. Zane furrowed his brows, looking at the elf and fae, but he was more concerned about checking on Hannah, who was thankfully still sound asleep. Zane was clueless about what was going on. After fixing the covers on Hannah and kissing her on the forehead, then walked out of her bedroom to see what the fuck happened.

"What the hell happened?" Zane growled.

"We had an intruder," Frost said.

"How?"

"They came in through Hannah's window," Ellie said. "I felt a change in the protection magic Frost had set around the house, and when I rushed upstairs to check, I saw someone leaning over Hannah. When I called out to them, they ran and knocked me out, and that's the last thing I remember. When I came to, Frost was helping me up, and they were gone."

Hannah was born hot-blooded, and even on the coldest nights, she likes to sleep with the window cracked to keep her cool.

"We should call the police," Zane said.

"There's no need," Frost interjected.

"What? Why?"

"Babe, did you forget what we are or who I know?"

Frost smiled. "You're a werewolf. Can't you sniff and see if you can pick out their scent?"

Zane furrowed his brows. *Why the hell didn't I think about that? People would think I wasn't an educated man.*

"It's okay; your main concern is Hannah," Frost said softly, then turned to Ellie. "You should head home and do your report, but please leave this part out. I don't need my parents showing up. If I need any help, I'll contact you."

"As you wish," Ellie said and then disappeared.

"Come on, let's see if we can find anything." Frost walked into Hannah's room and then over to her bed, waving a hand over her sleeping form. "Okay, I placed a barrier over her so we can move around without waking her."

Zane nodded and took off the blanket, shifting back into his wolf and searching around the room, not finding any new scents.

"Nothing is out of the ordinary, as far as I can tell," Zane said, shifting back to human and grabbing the blanket, wrapping it around his body.

"Same, from what I can tell," Frost said. "Not even a magical signature, so either the person is human, or they found a way to block me from figuring out who they are after they realized I'd set a protection on the house. Do you have any enemies?"

"Not ones that would try to enter my home." All of his enemies were in the business world and would attack his company, not his daughter. Of that Zane was certain.

"Let's check the rest of the house."

Frost nodded. "Okay."

They checked inside and out but found nothing. Not even a footprint.

"Whoever they are, they're pretty good, but I don't

think they'll return tonight. I set more protection around the house."

"You know I'm capable of protecting my daughter," Zane said, wincing at how snarky he sounded. "I'm sorry. I didn't mean for it to..."

"No, you're right. I overstepped my bounds," Frost said quickly. "I'm going to go."

Before Frost could get away, Zane grabbed his waist and pulled him close. "I'm sorry. I didn't mean for it to sound the way it did." He turned Frost around. "I've been a single father for so long, it's going to be hard for me to let some of that control go and allow you to be a full part of Hannah's life. Baby, forgive me."

"There's nothing to forgive." Frost leaned up and kissed him. "I'm going to go."

"Why?"

Frost stared into his face, not saying anything, and then it hit Zane. He never asked him to stay. *Fuck, Zane, you're an idiot. You're mates, not friends.*

Zane stepped back and grabbed Frost's hand, and after one more check on Hannah, he led him to the master bedroom. "This is the bathroom. There are extra tooth-brushes in the bottom drawer. Let me know if you use a special toothpaste, and I'll get it." He walked over to the closet where there was more than enough space for two, maybe three, people to hang as many clothes as they wanted, which he pointed out to Frost. "I like sleeping on the left side of the bed, but we can take turns if that's your preference. I'm not a morning person, but if you are, just keep it down. I like to sleep in the nude, but I always keep pajama pants close by in case Hannah happens to come into my room." Zane stopped speaking when he noticed Frost hadn't said anything but was simply staring at him. "What's the matter?"

"Are you asking me to spend the night with you or move in?"

"If I say both, what would be your answer? I'm not sure if we'll live here for the rest of our lives, but it's a start. This will be your home as well. Do whatever you feel like doing. So what do you think?"

"Stay right here. I'll be back."

Before his eyes, Frost disappeared, and Zane wondered what the fae was up to. He didn't have to wait long for Frost to return, holding an overnight bag and a pillow.

"I don't mind sleeping on the right side of the bed. And I can't sleep without my favorite pillow. Oh, and I got our things from the woods."

Zane had forgotten about his clothes from earlier, but that wasn't what he cared about. "Does that mean you are spending the night or moving in?"

"Both." Frost smiled.

"Come here." Frost dropped his things and moved into Zane's arms. "Despite what happened with the intruder, I had a good time tonight."

"Me too." He buried his head in Zane's chest.

"Come on, let's get to bed," Zane suggested.

"Okay."

CHAPTER ELEVEN

The following morning, Zane rolled over, running his hands over what should have been his mate sleeping beside him, only to come up short. He opened his eyes and sat up, looking around, disappointed that he was alone.

"Where are you?" Zane asked through their mental link.

"You're awake. Come down for breakfast. Hannah and I are waiting for you," Frost responded. *"Oh, and you have company."*

"Company?" Zane threw off the covers and got out of bed, wondering who it could be. After cleaning up and getting dressed, he headed downstairs but stopped when he felt he had walked into the wrong home. Zane remembered that Megan and Hannah had put up the Christmas tree, but he was trying to figure out how he'd gone to bed and woken up, and his home had been transformed into something new —red, white, and silver decorations with floating stars and snowflakes hanging from the ceiling.

Zane smiled as he walked further into his home, feeling a new change had occurred, and he could tell it was for the best. He hadn't seen Hannah, Frost, or the guest in any of the other rooms that seemed to have a theme to the new decorations, along with a Christmas tree to match, and if he wasn't paying attention, he might not have noticed the house seemed a tad bit bigger. Zane didn't have to think about who'd come up with the decorations. But the question Zane had been wondering was, *when did Frost have time to do this?* The closer he got to the kitchen, he finally heard Hannah and another person he recognized but was certain that it wasn't Frost laughing.

Megan, what is she doing here?

Zane walked into the kitchen and wasn't surprised to see Hannah and Megan sitting at the table working on something, but he couldn't tell what it was they were doing. But it was Frost who caught his eyes.

"Daddy, you're finally up," Hannah said excitedly, rushing over to hug him. "Did you see the new decorations? Frost and I did it. We had to be really quiet because we didn't want to wake you."

Zane wasn't sure what was happening. He was used to seeing Hannah with a game console attached to her hand before she even had breakfast, but there was none in sight.

"I saw them," he told Hannah, bending down and kissing her on the side of her head. "I like the new look."

"Hello, Zane."

He looked away from Hannah, and the smile slipped from his face. He wasn't sure why she was in his home. He thought he had made himself clear. "Megan, what are you doing here?" he asked, standing.

She smiled charmingly. "Your friend let me in."

Zane saw Frost's back stiffening from the corner of his eyes. Zane went to speak, but the doorbell rang.

"I'll get it," Frost said, hurrying out of the room without

looking in his direction. Hannah left Zane's side and followed after his mate.

Shit, what must he be thinking?

"Frost isn't just my friend; he's my lover," Zane said, setting things straight.

"Lover. When did you find time to get a lover? I was only gone for a couple of days. I thought if I gave you time to think things through you'd miss me, but..."

"Megan, where is all of this coming from?" he asked, cutting her off. "I was clear with you. I see you as a friend and nothing else."

"Why him and not me?" she asked, as if not hearing what he said.

Zane was certain that he hadn't given her any indication that he had feelings for her. "I think it's for the best if you stay away from Hannah and me from now on."

"Zane, don't do this," she begged.

"Please go, Megan." He felt like a broken record since they'd had this conversation before.

"Zane, we have more company," Frost's voice said from behind him, causing Zane to turn, ignoring Megan.

Zane's eyes widened when he faced a taller and slightly older version of Frost.

"Zane, I'd like for you to meet my big brother Nyx. I was trying to keep him away for one more day, but he never listens to me." Frost narrowed his eyes at his brother.

"I hope you don't mind me dropping by unannounced, but I think you should get used to it. Once the rest of the family finds out, you won't get a moment's peace."

Zane chuckled. "It's no problem."

"Don't you have something else to say to Zane?" Frost said, jabbing his elbow into his brother's side.

Nyx gritted his teeth. "Stop it," he said to Frost, who

listened. Then Nyx looked at Zane. "Hey, man, I'm sorry about the whole business thing. I wish I could say I wasn't going to take you down, but I was going to crush you for hurting him. As compensation, I brought this."

Nyx reached into his pocket and pulled out a stack of documents, handing it to Zane, who unfolded it, and his eyes widened when he read the first few lines. It was a partnership contract for SeRan Technologies. Zane had been trying to get a meeting with the CEO to discuss working together.

"How did you get this?"

"I pulled some strings," Nyx said, and a growl from Frost had him saying more. "Fine, I'm friends with Lim Dae-Ran, and I told him about your company. He said you've been trying to meet with him, and he looked over your portfolio and liked what he saw. I negotiated on your behalf, but if it's not up to your standards, we can work something out."

"No, this is fine. I'll have my lawyers look through the documents, but this is all good." Zane thought Nyx Winterbourne righting his wrong from before was enough. But if this deal was for real, he did more than enough. Business deal like this was one of the reasons Zane wanted to befriend Nyx, but it all worked out for the better now that he was Frost's mate.

"Okay, since that's settled, Frost, feed me," Nyx said.

"Feed yourself," Frost said, moving over to Zane who pulled him into his arms, and the pleasurable scent of mint and pine brushed against his nose. Zane had noticed Frost had two different scents. Mint and pine when he was happy and peaches and vanilla when he was aroused.

"Finally I get to hold you," Zane said, kissing his lips.

"Well, blame that on your friend Megan." Zane smiled, seeing Frost's lips curl in a snarl. "Anyway, where is she?"

Zane glanced around, noticing that Megan was nowhere to be found. "I think she left."

"I guess so," Frost said.

Looking at Frost, Zane put Megan out of his thoughts. He tilted his head and connected their lips together. He moaned, liking that his first sweet taste of the day was Frost. Zane held him close, forgetting where they were and simply enjoying his man.

"Ewww..." a childish and not-so-childish voice came behind them, causing him and Frost to break their kiss, turning to scowl at Nyx and Hannah staring at him.

"You two are ridiculous," Frost commented, stepping from his arms. "Sit down so we can eat."

"Daddy, I like Uncle Nyx and Frost," Hannah said, sitting beside him. "Uncle Nyx said anytime you and Frost get on my nerves to call him and he'll come and get me."

Zane looked at Nyx, who had just sat down at the table. "What did you give my kid to make her like you in a matter of minutes?"

Nyx smiled. "It's the Winterbourne charm. Get used to it. You're both a part of the family now." He shrugged. "Look, I've been waiting for Frost to give me a niece or nephew, and now that he has, I can spoil her to my heart's content. And when you have more kids, I'll do the same."

Zane shook his head, realizing he had gained a pack far quicker than expected. Minutes later, they started eating, and the conversation ran smoothly. Zane leaned back in his chair and listened to the Winterbourne brothers bicker between each other, bringing a delighted laughter from his daughter.

THE NEXT COUPLE of days were busy for Frost, with Lisa and Mark's wedding. Zane and Hannah were also in attendance as groomsmen and junior bridesmaids. Although Hannah looked so adorable, it was Zane who Frost couldn't take his eyes off. Dressed in a dark blue tuxedo with a blood-red tie, he looked utterly dashing to his eyes and others.

Once Frost had made sure everything was set and the dinner and speeches were done and he was about to walk through the door, he was grabbed around the waist and a muscular, solid chest pressed against his back.

"Where do you think you're going without saying goodbye to me?" Zane's warm breath tickled the outer part of his ear.

"Home."

"Want some company?"

Frost turned to face him. "Aren't you staying for the party?"

"If you're not here, how can I enjoy myself? Besides, I think we could have a different kind of party, especially on a night where the moon is full and bright. One where it involves me buried deep inside of you and you screaming my name," he whispered in a deep voice next to Frost's ear.

Frost quirked a brow. "I think you'll be the one calling out my name."

"Of that, I have no doubt. And before you asked about Hannah, I called in a favor, so we will be childless for the night."

"Who's watching Hannah? Not that Megan person." There was something about the lady Frost did not trust. Other than the fact that Hannah adored her, Frost didn't like the way Megan's eyes always followed Zane when she saw him. He would never admit that it was his jealousy speaking, but Frost felt there was something odd about her and he couldn't put his finger one it and was making sure to keep an eye on her. Frost had a feeling there was more to Megan than she was letting on.

Zane smirked. "I like it when you're jealous."

"I'm not jealous of anyone," Frost protested.

"Keep telling yourself that." Zane chuckled. "Anyway, I called your brother, and he agreed to watch Hannah for the night. We'll get her tomorrow before heading to Wynter Spell."

Other than preparing for the couple's wedding, Frost had told Hannah they would visit Frost's family, still keeping the secret that she would be meeting the famous Santa Claus. He could tell that she was nervous about the whole thing and he'd thought about skipping out on going to Wynter Spell that year. But when he explained they would be traveling on the magic train, the treats, and fun things she could do, Hannah grew excited, forgetting about her anxiety. However, that wasn't what was on Frost's mind at the moment.

"When did you and my brother get so friendly?"

"When he made me millions, after trying to bankrupt me."

Frost looked at Zane and mentally shook his head. Sometimes he thought his mate was far too nice. If he had been in the alpha's place, he would have plotted some horrible revenge on Nyx, even if his older brother was doing it as a favor to him.

"I know what you're thinking, and your brother is not so hard to get along with. He and I have a lot in common—you being the main one. And he admitted he wasn't going to let my company go belly up. Hell, I might seem nice all the time, but trust me, BM Technologies wasn't going to crumble," Zane explained, as if he had really read his mind. Even though they had opened a mental link, they learned to close off certain aspects of their thoughts. "Come on, how about you whisk us away to the Eclipse."

"The Eclipse?" He looked around, noting there were people walking around and knew how Zane felt when he used magic in front of unsuspecting humans.

"Yes." Zane took his hand and led him to one of the dark alcoves around where the wedding was held. "I can't wait any longer to make you my mate in every complete way."

Frost liked hearing that. They hadn't gone too far besides kissing and hand jobs. And although he enjoyed being next to Zane and being held in his arms as they slept, he wanted more.

"But why the Eclipse?"

"Even though I know you can put up a silencing barrier so Hannah won't hear us, for our first time, I want to concentrate on us."

Frost let out a mental sigh. He was glad it had nothing to do with Zane's late mate. He thought they hadn't made love yet because Zane didn't want to do it in the house he once shared with Arizona. But now, hearing the reasons, it settled Frost's heart. Frost had never been so patient in his life. When he saw something he wanted, he took it, but with Zane, he learned to hold back.

Not only that, he knew how kind-hearted Zane was, while Frost, on the other hand, was often seen as pushy. He thought they had made a great pair and had to thank fate for sending the right partner to him. Frost didn't waste any time, and they disappeared and appeared in Frost's bedroom at the Eclipse, falling on the bed in each other's embrace.

Their lips instantly found each other, and Frost poured out his feelings to the man in their kiss. Frost was in love with Zane and had always been, since the moment he saw the werewolf on the magazine cover. He loved everything about Zane, from the way he worried about and took care of his daughter to his earthy scent that always seemed to calm Frost when he got too anxious about things.

Zane separated from their kiss and leaned back, not taking his eyes off Frost. "Did I tell you how sexy you were tonight? You shine in your element," Zane said, unbuttoning his shirt. Frost shook his head no. "Well, you were. You're decisive in your actions and quick to fix any problems that come your way." He took off his shirt, throwing it to the floor.

Frost reached up and cupped one of Zane's cheeks. "Thank you."

"No need for thanks. It was a pleasure to watch you work."

Frost leaned up and connected their lips, drawing a hungry moan from Zane. Frost wrapped his legs around Zane's waist, pressing their hips together, regretting they were still wearing pants. A thought came to him, and with a wave of his hand, their clothes disappeared from their bodies, and he felt Zane smile in their kiss.

"I love it when you use your magic for good," Zane said against his lips.

"Always," Frost said, nipping at Zane's bottom lip.

Their hands roamed all over their bodies as their mouths devoured each other. Zane trailed open kisses down to Frost's neck, making him gasp when he scraped his canines across his skin, before moving down to his nipples, sucking, biting, and teasing them until they were red, hard pebbles and sensitive to the touch.

"Want you," Frost whimpered, carding his fingers through Zane's hair. "Don't make me wait any longer, please, babe."

———

ZANE RAISED his gaze to look into Frost's lustful and passion-filled eyes. He moved back up Frost's body and claimed his lips, feeding his hunger and desire into their kiss, hoping that his mate would feel it. Zane had grown frustrated trying to think of the perfect moment to claim Frost as his mate, but their bond was being stretched too thin. At Lisa's and Mark's wedding, Zane's eyes couldn't stop following the handsome fae.

Not only him but others as well, which played on Zane's jealousy and made him realize not only had he waited too long, but he'd gone from being fascinated and attracted to Frost to falling in love with the fae. Frost's hips jerked up, brushing their cocks together and bringing Zane back into focus. He reached down, grabbing Frost by his waist, grinding their hips together.

"Want to taste you," Zane whispered against his lips. "Give me your ass. I want to feast on it."

"Only if I can do the same to you," Frost said huskily.

"How can I refuse such sweet pleasures."

Zane flipped them over and positioned Frost on top of him. Frost turned around, putting his arse directly over Zane's face. He licked the corners of his mouth to stop himself from drooling when vanilla and peach scents filled his senses, arousing him even more. Zane grasped Frost's ass cheeks, kneading them and slapping the plump mounds a couple of times, loving how they instantly reddened. He wasn't a sadist, but he did take pleasure in teasing his lover into a maddening frenzy.

"Should I call you Daddy now, since it seems you like to spank me?" Frost said cheekily, but it turned into a whimper when he earned another swat on his ass. "I am definitely calling you Daddy from now on," he panted, wiggling his ass in front of Zane.

Zane smiled as he separated Frost's butt cheeks. Flattening his tongue, he dragged it across Frost's wet, slick hole, moaning at the sweet taste of his omega slick. His nails dug into Frost's flesh the more he tasted and knew he had found his new favorite dessert.

CHAPTER TWELVE

"Fuck," he moaned, feeling Zane's tongue press against his hole.

Frost wasn't a virgin by any means, but there were quite a few things he hadn't tried, like having his asshole rimmed, which was making him lose what was left of his mind. Frost wrapped his arms around Zane's muscled legs and opened them wider. He ran the tip of his nose along the veined shaft, breathing in his mate's earthy scent. He swirled his tongue around the head of Zane's cock, licking up his precum. Zane moaned, breathing against his hole, sending shivers up and down his spine.

Oh fuck, it feels so damn good.

Frost wrapped his lips around Zane's cock, sucking and jerking his erection. Frost jolted his hips when Zane inserted a finger in his hole while sucking Frost's balls into his mouth. Frost's cock rubbed against Zane's chest, leaving trails of precum. Frost reached between them, grabbing his cock, jerking himself in the same rhythm with the dick in his mouth.

His mate groaned, pivoting his hips, moving his cock in

and out of Frost's mouth as their passion intensified. Frost widened his legs when another finger entered his hole, and he swirled his hips, fucking Zane's hand and fingers in his asshole. Frost's pleasure heightened when Zane bit on one of his butt cheeks as he added another finger.

His lover's cock slipped from his mouth, unable to hold back his pleasurable moan. Frost reached back and widened his ass cheeks as far as they could go, grinding and swirling his waist as if guiding Zane's tongue and fingers to do his bidding.

Zane's large fingers stretched his hole, brushing on his prostate, making him lose his mind. Frost had never felt such pleasure before, and he couldn't stop his shift. His vision was so blurry he had to close his eyes, and his fangs pierced his tongue, filling his mouth with blood, trying to slow the process down, but it was no use.

Zane's tongue and fingers hadn't stopped moving. Frost gyrated his hips, moaning with each movement of Zane pleasuring him. Frost's cock was so hard he could feel his orgasm building, but he didn't want to tumble over the edge until he felt Zane's big cock pounding inside of him, with his canines nestled in his flesh, cementing their bond.

However, Zane's tongue and fingers hadn't slowed for a moment. It seemed as if his mate was hellbent on making him cum. He opened his eyes, noticing that the room was bathed in gray, his skin prickled with goose bumps, and his nails grew into claws. He arched his back, hoping to stop the itching where his wings sprouted since he felt like he was experiencing his first shift.

"Oh fuck, Zane. Baby, please, I need more," he begged. "I want to feel you inside of me."

But all he received for his fevered request was more pleasure.

Frost's senses were so heightened he couldn't stop what was happening. He looked over his shoulder and noticed that his alpha wasn't doing any better than he was. His nails had also shifted, and his canines were grazing against the sensitive parts of Frost's ass, sending waves of pleasure through him. Zane opened his eyes, and Frost gasped, seeing the hungry desire in the man's gaze, almost causing Frost's heart to stop.

Zane looked as if he wanted to consume him as his last meal. This scared Frost as much as it excited him that Zane wanted him so badly.

ZANE GAZED into Frost's eyes and knew Frost had no clue how fucking sexy he looked at this moment. Frost's eyes were filled with want for him, to the point of almost being feral. Zane carefully removed his fingers, and with one last lick of his mate's sweet hole, Frost turned around. Zane grabbed him by the back of his neck, pulling him and claiming his swollen lips in a sensual kiss.

He rolled them over, trailed his lips down Frost's neck, and moved down to his nipples. "You are so damn delicious. I could spend my days licking you all over."

Frost smirked. "You can do anything you want to me."

Zane raised his head. "Don't say it like that. I might take things too far."

Frost cupped his mate's cheek. "You can never go too far."

Zane growled deep and low, running a clawed finger down his chest as he claimed a nipple between his sharp canines. Frost shivered, cupping the back of his head. Zane could tell Frost was holding back his shift, and truthfully, so was he. The magic of the full moon was begging him to claim his mate, and it was one request Zane didn't not plan on rejecting. This was the first time he'd ever been so aroused he'd wanted to fuck his mate, wanting to let his wolf out.

"Don't hold back your shift," Zane said, licking the red hardened nub. "I want to see the real you."

Frost grabbed his hair and lifted his head. "Are you sure?"

Zane moved up his body so that they were eye to eye. "No hiding from each other," he told him, partially shifting. Short gray hair sprinkled all over his shoulders, upper arms, and parts of his legs. He could feel his ears and tail coming out and the other changes.

Frost peered into his face, raising a hand to caress it, running a thumb over his lips. "Fuck, you're beautiful."

Zane kissed his finger. "You are, too." Leaning down, he pressed their mouths together. Frost gasped, hugging Zane's neck with one hand and moving the other to play with his tail, making him shiver with need. Their kiss was slow, filled with so much passion that it often had Zane gasping for breath. Every touch, every moan, every whimper heightened their passion.

Frost's fingers roughly ran through Zane's fur. Their teeth clashed against each other, scraping and breaking the skin, unable to tell whose blood they were tasting. Their scents and pheromones flooded the room, along with their magic, and Zane could feel the threads of their bond coming together.

Frost's arms tightened around his body, and before he knew it, Zane was flipped on his back. Frost leaned back, pressing his palms into Zane's chest and gazing down into his face.

"I need you inside of me now."

"Then take me," Zane told him.

Raising his hips, Frost reached behind him and grasped Zane's cock. Zane pulled Frost's ass cheeks apart and groaned, feeling the head of his cock pressing against his mate's slick hole. They both moaned and shivered when his erection entered Frost's hole.

"Zane," Frost hissed, pressing down and taking more of Zane's cock.

Zane wasn't doing any better. "Fuck, baby, your ass is so damn tight. I love it."

Frost pressed his palms into Zane's chest and swirled his hips, moving down until they were ass to pelvis. Frost's hole had Zane's cock in a vice grip, but he couldn't deny how good he felt. Zane squeezed and kneaded Frost's ass, hoping it would help him to relax his hold a bit.

"Move, baby," he said once Frost loosened up.

Frost moaned and leaned forward, raising up his ass before slamming down. Zane released a feral growl at how good it felt.

"Fuck, yes," Frost panted breathlessly, doing the same move once again. His nails turned into claws and dug into Zane's chest, breaking the skin. Frost ground his hips, riding Zane, who was meeting him thrust for thrust. As their bodies came together in an intimate dance, the markings appeared on Frost's body, his hair grew in length, and his eyes seemed to glow, aided by the moonlight coming into the room. Watching Frost's body transform made Zane's gums and teeth ache and burn to bite and claim him completely, but not yet; he wanted Frost in a frantic need.

Zane's heart thundered in his chest as the fire in his body burned like a volcano, ready to erupt. Grabbing Frost's hips, Zane steadied the man's waist, pulling back until his cock was almost out before thrusting deep and hard into him. Frost screamed, throwing his head back as his wings sprang from his back.

Loving the reaction, Zane did it a couple more times, watching Frost turn into a feral, needy fae.

"Zane...oh fuck...fuck me harder," he chanted. "Tear me apart, mark me..." His words became a mantra that Zane could not deny.

Zane couldn't take it anymore and pulled Frost off his cock and flipped him onto his hands and knees. Before Frost could muster a protest, Zane separated the fae's ass cheeks, slipping a thumb into his stretched hole.

"Going to fuck you until you can't walk," Zane growled, gripping his cock and positioning it to Frost's hole. Removing his thumb, he pushed in all the way, not allowing the fae to adjust. Zane thrust deep and long, pegging his prostate. Frost arched his back, and his wings fluttered loudly in the room, mixing with the throaty groans and moans. Magic and lust filled the room as he fucked his love with abandon, claiming what was rightfully his.

"Zane...yes...fuck...right there," sprang from Frost's mouth in no particular order.

Zane's claws dug into Frost's hips, and his canines grew longer, trying to pull out the tiny lykosian gene buried deep inside him. Zane's thrusts grew more intense, and the sound of skin smacking against each other ricocheted off the room walls. The bed creaked and bounced with his movement. That feral need in Zane rose even higher the deeper he thrust his cock.

"Mine," Zane growled. "You are mine."

Grabbing Frost by the front of his neck, he pulled him, pressing their hot sweaty skin together. They both moaned at the change in positions.

Zane grasped Frost's cock, stroking in the same rhythm as his hips pistoning inside of him, licking and then dragging his teeth, breaking the skin on the side of his neck. Blood slowly trickled out of the wound, marring Frost's creamy skin, giving him a beautiful blush.

"Who do you belong to?" Zane demanded. "Say it!"

Frost's wings fluttered around then, as if it was the only way he could use words, since he seemed a bit tongue-tied. Zane lapped at the blood on his neck, moaning at the sweet taste.

"Are you ready to be mine, little fae?"

Frost's wings wildly fluttered, and he pressed his head into Zane's chest, gasping. Their bodies moved in sync as magic continued to swirl around them.

"Z...Zane..." he moaned, slurring his words like a drunken man. "C...cum."

Zane couldn't take it anymore and sank his canines into Frost's neck.

"Zane!" Frost screamed, and his tight ass clamped down on Zane's cock, cumming on his hand. His hips stuttered but did not stop. He could feel his orgasm skirting on the edge.

He moaned when blood gushed into his mouth. He shivered, feeling their bond locking into place, and the longing that had settled in his heart disappeared. His canines dug deep into his neck, and with one last thrust, he erupted like a volcano, cumming and searing and marking Frost's channel. Zane grunted as his knot formed, locking them together. The wild sex magic wrapped around them, embracing them like a warm blanket. After a few minutes, he removed his canines, licked the bite wound, and was pleased when it didn't heal right away. They slowly fell on the bed, panting and gasping for air.

Zane rolled Frost onto his stomach, kissing his shoulder and back. Frost moaned when Zane ground his knot against his prostate and reached back to grab his hips. He turned his head, and their eyes locked on each other, and an unspoken understanding passed through them. Their lovemaking session was not over. Zane leaned down and captured his mouth, and started fucking him once more.

FROST HUMMED, lying across Zane's chest, cuddled in his mate's arms. They had made sweet love all night, and Zane had left him completely satisfied. He was sore everywhere that counted. Although he could heal his body with magic, he didn't want to. He wanted to feel and see Zane's marks on him.

"What are you smiling about?" Zane asked in a deep voice above his head.

"How good you made me feel tonight," Frost answered truthfully.

"Who says the night is over?" Zane rolled on top of him and kissed his lips sweetly.

"I don't want this night to end," Frost said when their lips separated. They were mates now, and he felt their magic swirling around them. He felt so connected to Zane and did not want to leave the cocoon of his embrace.

"Baby, we have the rest of our lives to recapture this moment."

Frost smiled. "I like the sound of that."

"Me too." Their lips met once more, and although Frost would like them to make love again, he was satisfied with them simply holding each other as they fell asleep.

FROST CHUCKLED, watching the wonderment on Hannah's face. They'd returned to Zane's home in time to retrieve Hannah and their luggage and catch the magic train. It had been a while since he had taken the train. Unlike most, Frost liked traveling between the realms since it was much faster and easier. But because Zane and Hannah knew nothing about the realms, he figured the train was the best option. Although Frost knew that one day, he would need to explain the whole thing to Zane, since his office building used realm magic.

Frost couldn't blame Hannah if she felt a bit over-whelmed by everything that she was seeing. The train offered a lot to keep passengers entertained during the ride. Other than the ever-changing scenery, there were a couple of dining cars, shifters walking around in their animal forms, a marketplace, a park, magically enlarged compart-ments, not to mention the secret car with more children's letters to his uncle Nick, and many other fun things to do.

Frost did wonder, with a child who had magic surrounding her, why she did not believe that Santa Claus was real.

"Are you having fun, little witchlet?"

Frost had given her the nickname because she was a witch, and he could see small bursts of magic sparkling around her. It was a wonder she hadn't had any magical outbursts yet. Frost could only guess it had something to do with her being part werewolf.

"Yes, I'm having lots of fun. Magic is so awesome," she said, pointing to the floating tray filled with sweet treats and drinks. "Can you make things float too, Frost?"

"Of course, and so will you one day," Frost told her. He

was trying to broach the subject of not believing in Santa but didn't want to give too much away.

"Baby girl, even with all of this, you still don't think Santa Claus is real?" Zane asked, picking up on Frost's train of thought.

"Daddy, let's not go through this again," Hannah said exaggeratedly. "Just because magic is real, that doesn't mean he is."

What an intelligent child!

"I think by the end of the night, you'll change your mind," Frost simply said, seeing that nothing he said would ever change her mind.

Hannah narrowed her eyes. "What do you mean by that?" she huffed, looking at Zane when Frost didn't respond. "Daddy, what's Frost talking about?"

Zane shrugged his shoulders, chuckling when she became minimally annoyed with their actions. "All I can say is it's a surprise, and you must wait and see. I'm kind of excited about the whole thing myself."

"You know it's not cool that parents keep secrets from their innocently naive children," she grumbled.

Both Zane and Frost laughed. "Just be patient," Frost told her. "We'll be in Wynter Spell soon, and then you'll know what I'm talking about." He waved the tray over to Hannah, and her face brightened instantly. She started eating, seeming to forget about the surprise.

"You're good with her," Zane whispered in his ear.

"Thank you. I like her and want to be a good parent to her."

"You will be." He kissed Frost on the cheek. "Just give it time. I think after tonight, you will be her favorite person."

"Nah, I think that honor will go to my uncle Nick. Oh, when you meet him, don't call him SC. He hates it when adults do that." Frost had told Zane the surprise he had planned for Hannah to meet his Uncle Nick.

"Okay, thanks for the tip." Zane chuckled. "I don't want to get on anyone's bad side on our first meeting."

"You won't. They'll love you. You already got past my brother."

"We'll see," Zane said, not sounding convinced.

"You'll do fine," he told him, then rested his head on Zane's shoulder, settling in for the rest of the ride, thankful that Nyx had decided to sit in another compartment with a few friends he'd met up with, so the new family of three had time to get to know each other.

CHAPTER THIRTEEN

They pulled up to Frost and Nyx's family home a couple of hours later after getting off the train. Frost got out of the car and breathed in the fresh air. It hadn't been that long since he'd been home, but every time he visited, he felt rejuvenated. Sometimes, he hated leaving. Maybe Bronwyn was right and he should just move back to Wynter Spell, but then, Frost could visit whenever he wanted, so it wasn't a complete loss.

"So, where is your house?" Zane said, coming to stand beside him.

Frost smiled. "Come on, I'll show you." Frost grabbed his and Hannah's hand, guiding them up to the house. He smiled when Hannah grasped, knowing what caught her eyes. It was kind of hard to miss the enormous treehouse that was Frost's family home.

"It's a treehouse," Hannah said excitedly.

"Your family home is a treehouse, seriously?" Zane asked. "I was expecting a mansion like the Eclipse."

Frost chuckled. "Don't judge a tree by its branch."

As it was called, the Lantern had been in the Winterbourne family since the beginning of Wynter Spell. It might've looked small on the outside but was quite large on the inside. There was something special about the homes in town. Not only were they magically enhanced, but the houses were either made in or built around a tree, keeping the roots and branches intact. The base and foundation of the Lantern was a Chapel Oak that was commonly grown in France, and was tall and majestic.

However, just like everything in Wynter Spell, it bent the rules of nature. Over the years, the branches had grown more extensive and robust to hold the lanterns named after each Winterbourne family member. Thanks to magic and love, the leaves had grown greener. With the growth of their family, his parents added more rooms to the Lantern, as evidenced by the extra lit window up in the left corner of the tree.

"Come on. Let's go meet the family," Frost said, pulling them up the stairs and over the bridge connecting to the Lantern and opening the door. They were instantly greeted by the scent of freshly baked cookies and cakes.

"Mom, we're home," Nyx called out and went to the kitchen, leaving Zane, Frost, and Hannah behind.

The second he stepped inside, Frost was pulled into a bone-crushing hug. "You're finally here!"

"Bronwyn, you're killing me," Frost wheezed. He wasn't surprised that Bronwyn was at his family home. It wasn't just her but her mate and the rest of her family.

She stepped back and eyed him suspiciously, then looked at Zane. "I see why you're late. Usually, you'd have been here as soon as Auntie Bell broke out the butter to make your favorite cookies."

"We took the train so Hannah could experience the ride," Frost explained.

"Hannah?" Bronwyn said, confused.

Frost stepped to the side so his best friend could see Zane's daughter.

"Well, aren't you a pretty little witchlet?" Bronwyn gushed, kneeling in front of Hannah. "I'm Bronwyn Read, but you can call me Auntie when you're ready."

Hannah extended a hand like she did when she had introduced herself to Ellie, and Bronwyn squealed. "Oh, Grand-Odin, she is adorable, Frost."

Frost smiled, ruffling Hannah's hair.

"Are you ready to meet Sa—"

Frost and Zane cleared their throat loudly, stopping Bronwyn from giving away the surprise Frost had set up. Bronwyn looked at them, and Frost shook his head, mouthing *"It's a surprise."* Her eyes widened, and then she smiled.

"As I was saying, are you ready to meet the rest of the family?"

Hannah, seeming not to catch on, nodded.

"Come on." Bronwyn stood and held out her hand to Hannah. "I'll introduce you to them while your daddies put your bags away."

Bronwyn and Hannah went off to the kitchen, and Frost turned to look at Zane. "Want the tour or to meet the family first?"

"Tour first," Zane said.

"Don't tell me you're nervous about meeting my family." Frost smiled and stepped closer to him.

"No...well, kind of."

"I understand, but don't worry, they will love you." He reached up and kissed Zane. It was supposed to be a short kiss, but once he touched Zane's lips, he could not pull away, and their mouths melded together. Zane's arms circled his waist, pulling him flush against his body. Frost moaned when Zane's tongue swept into his mouth, claiming him and sending fire throughout him. Frost wasn't sure how long they had stood at the door kissing, but neither seemed to want to move, even with the cold winds blowing against them. They were too focused on each other's lips.

"Well, now I know why the house has a slight draft."

Frost and Zane stopped kissing when he heard his mother's voice behind him. Clearing his throat, Frost stepped away from Zane and hugged his mother. "Hey, Mom," he said, kissing her snow-white hair that resembled his own.

"Hello, my sweet son," she said, kissing Frost on the cheek, then stepped back to look at him. "You look happy."

"I am."

"Good." She smiled.

Frost looked around, not seeing his dad, who would never leave his mother alone for too long. "Where's Dad?"

"He's still at the Workshop with your uncle. We'll meet up with him later. Now, introduce me to your mate."

Frost nodded and went over to Zane, who had closed the door. He grabbed the man's hand, pulling him over to her. "Zane, I'd like for you to meet the special lady in my life, Bell Boroson-Winterbourne, my mother. Mom, this is my mate, Zane Blood-Moon," Frost said proudly.

Bell stared up at Zane for a few minutes before she motioned for him to lean down, which he did without question. Bell touched his cheek. "You don't need to worry anymore, my child. Your Arizona is happy you've opened your heart again. She has finally moved on." Bell pulled Zane into her little arms. "You have a pack now."

Zane gasped and looked at Frost. "*Did you tell her about Arizona?*"

Frost shook his head. *"My mother is one of a handful of people who can speak to the dead."*

"Don't you think that's something you should have mentioned?"

"I had no idea she would say that, honest."

Zane nodded, seeming to be satisfied with the answer, but Frost knew he would have to explain things later. After a few minutes, they pulled apart.

"And don't blame Frost for not telling you about my abilities; there are some things he cannot reveal without our permission. But you'll find out everything as time goes on."

Zane sighed and nodded.

"Good," Bell said. "Come on, let's eat. We have a festive night ahead of us."

She left them alone, and Zane moved closer to him. "I take it the secrets left to tell are far bigger than your uncle being Santa Claus?"

"Yes."

"Okay," Zane said after a few moments. "I must admit I'm feeling somewhat overwhelmed and haven't even taken my coat off yet. So take all the time you need to let things out slowly."

"You're a good and understanding man, Zane Blood-Moon. It's why I lo—like you so much," Frost said, hoping Zane didn't catch his slip-up. "Let's go before my mom comes back, looking for us. Later, I'll give you a tour."

Frost walked off before Zane could say anything else, but before he could get too far, a strong arm circled his waist, pulling him back, and turned him around. "Never hold back on saying what you feel, and neither will I." He took a deep breath and gazed into Frost's face. "I love you too, Frost."

Frost's heart caught in his chest as he stared into the

man's beautiful eyes, seeing the truth. He was so overjoyed. "I love you, Zane."

Their lips met in a heated kiss, and instead of going to the kitchen to eat with the others, Frost teleported them to his bedroom, knowing that he'd have to apologize to his mother later, but right then and there, he needed to be with his mate.

"I WOULD THINK BEING in the middle of the North Pole I'd be freezing my a...butt off," Zane said, a couple of hours later, as he, Frost, and Hannah walked to the stables hand in hand.

"That's because of the magic surrounding Wynter Spell. It's the same one that hides Vale Valley and Valley-wood, but then with something extra added to it," Frost explained, looking at him, and the interest must have shown on his face. "Wish magic."

"Wish magic?" Hannah asked.

"Yes." Frost kneeled in front of her. "All the wishes worldwide that are fulfilled help keep this place safe."

"Why here?" Hannah asked. "And who are they making their wishes to?"

Frost smiled and stood. "Come with me. There's someone I want to introduce you to."

He took her hand and led them both into the stables that housed nine stalls, with the same number of beautiful animals with the most majestic antlers Zane had ever seen. Granted, he knew this surprise was for Hannah, but he couldn't help feeling just as anxious and awed at what he saw.

"Are those reindeer?" Hannah said, the wonder not missed from her tone.

"Mmm-hmm. Why don't you take a look at their names and tell me if you recognize any of them," Zane suggested.

She looked up at Zane with her bright eyes that reminded him of her mother, and he could see her apprehension and curiosity.

"Go on," he encouraged, and she nodded. Releasing Frost's hand, Hannah walked over to the first stall and read the first name out loud.

"Prancer," she said, then moved to the next stall, doing the same with the rest, but paused when reaching the last one, noticing that his nose turned red before she said his name.

HANNAH GASPED as realization hit her. Maybe it had long ago, but it wasn't until she reached Rudolph's stall that it made her stop and look at her father and Frost.

"Why do they have the names of Santa Claus's reindeer?" she asked her father, who turned to look at Frost.

The fae, as she'd come to know him, walked over and touched her shoulder. "Because that's what my uncle Nick named them. And Rudolph here is the star of the bunch."

At hearing that, the other reindeer snorted and scraped their hoofs on the straw, showing their displeasure at Frost's words.

"Oh, don't you lot be jealous. You know the truth." Frost snickered. "But I will admit they are all important. Do you remember when I told you that all the fulfilled wishes keep Wynter Spell safe?"

Hannah stared up at Frost, wondering what he and her daddy were up to. She'd liked the man from the first time they met at her Auntie Lisa and Uncle Mark's house. Hannah also noticed that there was something different about the man. He used a lot of magic around her, making her feel safe and comfortable. She knew Frost was her daddy's mate, and he had never made her feel worried he did not want her around, including her in everything. Also, since coming to Wynter Spell, Hannah had thought this was where she belonged.

Hannah finally nodded.

"Well, when the wishes come to Wynter Spell, they are delivered to a certain person. Can you guess who that is?"

Hannah instantly shook her small head because she had no clue.

"They come to me," said a booming voice that had Hannah rushing to grab Frost's legs and burying her face to hide her surprise. Hannah was not one of those kids who was scared easily, but the man's voice was strong and minimally deeper than her daddy's.

"It's okay," Frost soothed, chuckling. "This is my uncle Nick."

"I didn't mean to scare you, little Hannah Blood-Moon." His tone was softer and less scary.

Hannah slowly peeked from around Frost's legs and stared at the tall man, who seemed a couple of inches taller than her daddy. He had dark hair and bright blue eyes and wore a sleeveless red vest that stopped at his knees, matching red pants, black boots, and a black belt around his waist.

Under the vest, he wore a white shirt. If Hannah didn't know any better, she would have thought he was the mythical Santa Claus she used to believe in, but since she was all grown up, she no longer held such childish beliefs. Also, according to everything she knew about Santa Claus, he had a round belly, glasses that rested above his rosy cheeks, his famous white hair, and he had a touch of brown.

"You're not real," she said, unable to stop herself.

"Maybe this will convince you, little Hannah Blood-Moon."

As he said the words, the man's appearance changed, taking on Santa Claus's appearance with all she had imagined with the rotund stomach, the blushed cheeks, white hair and beard with brown touches, his eyes that were already blue seemed even brighter all that was missing was the glasses sitting on the bridge of his nose. Seeing it all was causing serious doubt in Hannah's mind.

Maybe he's a werewolf like my daddy?

The man chuckled, and it brought a good feeling to Hannah. "I am not a werewolf," he said, shocking her as if he read her thoughts, then his face grew serious. "I know why you don't believe in me, Hannah." He reached into his top left vest pocket and pulled out an envelope. Hannah recognized the handwriting—it was hers and the only letter she had written and mailed to Santa years earlier without her daddy knowing. "I'm sorry I was late in fulfilling your wish. But I had to wait for fate to take its course and for your dad to open his heart. I'm sorry it took me so long, Hannah, but matters of the heart are complicated, and I hope you can forgive me."

Hannah wanted to hold on to her doubts until the man dressed as Santa moved over to her and pulled Hannah into his arms, whispering the one thing she'd wished for when she asked for her daddy to find love.

"Frost and your daddy will live happily for a very, very long time. You don't have to be afraid because no one will die and leave you alone."

"You can't promise that," Hannah choked, trying not to cry.

"Yes, I can," he said firmly, and somehow, Hannah believed him.

Tears clouded Hannah's eyes, and she wrapped her arms around the man, whispering, "Santa Claus."

CHAPTER FOURTEEN

Zane watched his daughter melt in Nick's arms as he comforted her. Zane had heard the last part of what Nick had said to Hannah and had no clue she feared being alone. She was barely three years old when Arizona died, and he thought he was doing his best, letting her know he would always be there for her. But all he could do from now on was keep trying.

He looked at Frost when he squeezed his hand. "She will be all right."

"I know," Zane said.

Just as he spoke, the stable doors opened and a man who resembled Frost but with raven hair like Nyx entered carrying a red bag lined with fur. A few other people followed him. Frost released his hand and ran over to the man.

"Dad," he shouted, jumping into the man's arms, who, it seemed, was expecting him and caught the small fae easily.

It brought a smile to Zane's face, watching his mate act childlike, being held by his father. A few minutes later, Frost walked over and introduced them.

Rowan Winterborne was a whiz but later turned his multi-billion company over to his son and disappeared from the business world. Truthfully, Zane hadn't thought about the man, even after he met Frost.

"Daddy, Santa said I can go with him to deliver the presents, but only if you say yes," Hannah said, pulling him from his thoughts.

"Uh..." Zane froze, not sure what to say.

"That's great, witchlet," Frost took over for him. "It's fun. I did it when I was a wee little fae." He turned to Zane. "She will be safe, and a couple of other elf helpers will go along, and before you ask, magical seat belts are a must."

"So can I?" She looked up at him with bright eyes and a face he couldn't say no to, and he simply nodded his head.

"Yes," she cheered, hugging him quickly.

"So, you believe in Santa Claus now?"

"Yup."

"Good," Zane said. "No matter how or what happens, never give up on your beliefs."

"Okay, Daddy." She turned and looked at Frost. "Thank you, Frost, for introducing me to your uncle Nick."

"You're welcome, witchlet. Now run along. It's time for him to take off. If I'm not mistaken, they have a special helper's outfit for you."

She nodded and ran off and was helped up on the sleigh that had been pulled into the stables while they were talking. Zane wasn't sure what was happening, but it seemed he was very trusting of Frost's family, as if knowing they would never let anything happen to Hannah, and that made him feel great.

"Come on, we should join the others."

"Others?" Zane questioned.

Frost pulled him out of the stables, and he saw a crowd

of people congregating together, while others were walking by an enormous globe that lit up with colors that resembled the aurora borealis. Not only that but the globe looked very familiar.

"I've seen that before," he said, pointing to the globe.

"You have. Only that is a different one. That one belongs to my uncle Nick. Remember how I told you that former residents return to Wynter Spell to lend their magic on Christmas Eve? Well, when you touch the globe, it pulls away just one percent of your magic, and it helps him travel around the world. Once he collects the magic, he shrinks the globe and locks it into the sled's navigation. When he comes home, the magic is returned to you."

"Interesting."

Zane walked over to the globe and grazed his hand over it, and it turned the color of a full moon before going back to its original state. He smiled, feeling good to have contributed to helping someone's wish come true. Not more than ten minutes later, everyone watched as Nick, along with his helpers, took to the air. Hannah was all smiles as she waved to everyone on the ground. Everyone cheered when Nick called out all the names of the reindeer and flew off in the blink of an eye.

"So, since we're childish for a few hours, what do you want to do?" Zane asked.

Frost hummed and wrapped his arms around his neck. "I could think of a few things." He leaned up to kiss Zane but stopped, slipped out of his arms, grabbed a handful of snow, and threw it at a shocked Zane.

"Oh, so that's how it's going to be," he said, chuckling.

He reached down and gathered some snow and threw it at Frost who ducked, and it ended up hitting an unsus-pecting Rowan. Zane was about to apologize, only to hear someone shout "Snowball fight!" and a flurry of snow flew every which way, causing Zane to run, grabbing a cackling Frost and ducking behind the stables.

"I should get you back for throwing snow in my face," he said.

"But you won't." Frost smiled, wrapping his arms around his neck.

"No." He circled Frost's waist, leaning down and brushing their lips together. "I'd rather do this," he said, capturing Frost's lips and kissing him deeply as the laughter and the happiness added to their love and happiness.

A FEW DAYS LATER, back at home, Zane woke up in the dead of night because he felt something was off. Getting out of bed, Zane pulled on his pajama pants and then went to check on Hannah who was fast asleep. They still hadn't caught the intruder, and Zane was still worried about who they might be. He checked the windows, making sure they were locked. Zane had done something he should have done long ago, investing in an air conditioner that was only for Hannah's room.

Moving back over to Hannah's bedside, he readjusted her covers and then left, heading to his office since he was unable to sleep. They had returned home from Wynter Spell after having a wonderful Christmas. Hannah had been on cloud nine since helping Nick deliver presents on Christmas Eve and hadn't stopped talking about all the things she had seen.

On Christmas Day, the entire family sat down for breakfast before they opened presents and played games, then everyone took part in preparing dinner before settling down. It was a new thing for Zane and Hannah, who'd only had each other for so long. Sure, they visited Arizona's family, but it was usually long after the holidays.

Zane sat at his desk, and just as he was about to start working, he looked up when he heard Frost's voice.

"Couldn't sleep?"

"Sort of."

"Why didn't you wake me?" he asked, moving over to Zane who pushed his chair back just in time for Frost to straddle his legs. "I could have found ways to tire you out."

Zane quirked a brow. "Really?"

"Oh yes," Frost whispered, claiming his lips.

Zane moaned the second their mouths touched. He loved kissing Frost. The man's mouth was plump, soft, and firm. He delved his tongue inside his mate's hot mouth, taking all he could and giving his everything to Frost. His hands roamed all over Frost, kneading and caressing his ass, wanting and needing to be inside his lover. Slowly, their lips separated, and their eyes opened as they panted for breath.

"I want yo..."

Zane didn't let Frost finish his words. He stood with Frost in his arms and hurried back to their room. Frost peppered kisses on his neck. Once he reached the bedroom, he set Frost down on his feet and pressed his lips to Frost's, taking another kiss. Zane shoved his pants down as he slowly backed them up toward the bed. He pulled away from Frost for only a little bit to take off his night clothes.

"I need to be inside of you now," Zane growled.

Frost moaned and licked his lips. The look in his man's bright blue eyes spoke so many volumes; Zane was glad they were all for him, making him even more eager to feel Frost's warmth surrounding him. Once they were both naked, he captured Frost's lips in another searing-hot kiss. He groaned when their hot flesh came into contact. He lowered Frost to the bed, not once separating their lips.

Zane reached between them, taking Frost's cock into his hand, jerking it lightly, trailing his tongue down to his neck and then to one of his nipples before sucking it into his mouth. His thumb swiped at the head of Frost's cock, and he smiled when the man's body quivered under his touch. He licked his way over to the other nipple and did the same thing as he'd done to the first, making them both hard and red.

"Fuck, Zane, stop teasing me."

"What do you want?" he asked around the nipple he had just swirled his tongue around.

"You, in me."

Zane raised his head and looked into Frost's eyes. "If you want me so bad, prepare yourself for me."

Frost gasped and licked his fingers. Zane leaned back on his knees as his mate widened his legs and then pressed two of his fingers into his hole, groaning and grinding his hips.

He moaned, leaning in and licking his way down Frost's chest, stopping to kiss and suck up marks on his stomach, before moving down further and swallowing his hard cock in his mouth. Frost whimpered, calling his name. His hand gripped the back of his head with his free hand and jerked his hips up, sending his cock further into Zane's mouth. Zane moaned, bobbing his head up and down, sucking Frost's cock down even further.

Zane fondled Frost's balls, brushing a finger against his perineum, making him moan and groan. Frost added another finger to his hole and widened his legs as his nails dug further into Zane's flesh, causing him to wince, but that did not stop him from what he wanted. Pulling off Frost's cock, he licked and sucked his balls before making his way further down, slipping his tongue in and out of the crack of his ass, joining his mate's fingers. Zane wanted just a little taste. His tongue moistened Frost's hole and fingers, and it was fine for a little while, until he grew greedy and wanted more.

"Zane, babe," Frost panted. "Need you."

"You have me, baby."

He leaned back and removed Frost's fingers, inserting three of his own, moving them in and out. Frost ground his ass on Zane's fingers, fucking himself hard. Zane grasped his cock, jerking it a few times while he fucked Frost with the fingers still inside him.

When he knew that his man was close to cumming, Zane removed his fingers from the other man's ass, gripping Frost's hip as he lined the head of his cock against Frost's ass, teasingly fucking his cheeks without pushing it directly into his hole, before slowly pushing the head of his cock into Frost's greedy hole.

"Zane," Frost moaned as his hands went above his head and grabbed onto the bed railings, wrapping his legs around Zane, digging his heels into Zane's ass, and started moving his hips.

"Oh fuck, babe, you feel so fucking good."

Zane moved his cock in and out of Frost slowly. But the heat building between them wouldn't allow him to be gentle. He grunted and pistoned his hips, fucking Frost, piercing and marking the man's skin with his nails, praying to all the gods that they don't heal right away. He wanted to see Frost wearing his marks. Their moans filled the room, and Zane hoped Frost had remembered to set the silencing charm on the room because he was too far gone in their lovemaking to stop.

"Zane, fuck me harder," Frost babbled. "Need it harder."

He was never one to leave a lover wanting. Zane released Frost's hips and reached up for his ankles. He widened his legs as far as they could go and fucked his lover with wild abandon.

"Like that?" he growled.

Frost grunted and nodded, begging for more. Zane didn't stop Frost when he reached for his cock, jerking it in rhythm with how he was being fucked.

"Cumming," Frost whimpered, clamping down on Zane's cock as ropes of cum squirted on his stomach, chest, and the bottom of his chin.

Zane wasn't doing any better. His hips stuttered at seeing the beautiful sight, and he didn't have time to warn his mate as he felt the first burst of his cum rush from his cock, searing Frost's walls. He let out a long and pleasurable moan, and his body stilled, knotting Frost. He slowly released Frost's legs and fell forward, claiming Frost's lips in a sloppy kiss, feeling drunk with pleasure and greedy for more.

"I want more," he moaned.

"Then take me."

There was nothing that needed to be said. Zane spent more hours making sweet love to his mate as they claimed each other repeatedly.

FROST HUMMED, rolling over and waking up from a beautiful dream. He burrowed his head in the mounds of pillows, searching for Zane's warmth. They'd made love for hours the night before, and Frost was disappointed that he had to go to work while Hannah and Zane got to stay home and have fun. Although he was the boss, he had a couple of other functions to organize before the year ended. He felt the bed dip, and soft kisses on his shoulder had him peeking slightly from under the pillows.

"It's time to get up, baby."

Frost groaned. "I don't want to. I'm calling in sick."

"It's not good to lie. What will Hannah think if she finds out her new best friend is a liar?"

Since going to Wynter Spell, Hannah had been sticking to him and asking him questions about his childhood and when they would revisit the magical town. He didn't mind answering her questions. He was delighted that she was interested in getting to know him more. He dug his head deeper into the mattress, hoping to disappear.

"It's not fair." He raised his head, pouting.

Zane chuckled. "No, it's not, but would it make you feel any better that I will also be here working? The only person having fun will be Hannah."

"Maybe a little," Frost said, still not sounding happy.

Zane leaned down and kissed him, then leaned back. "What time is your last meeting?"

"Around four."

"Okay, we'll meet for dinner, how does that sound?"

"Hmm...I'd prefer staying home, but I can handle that option."

"Good. Get up. Breakfast is ready."

Frost smiled. "What a good mate you are. Maybe you should think about being a house husband instead of a world-class CEO."

"It is a thought," Zane said, walking out of the bedroom and leaving Frost to get ready for work.

After sitting down and having a good meal with

Hannah and Zane, he was out the door. When he got to work, Bronwyn was already there.

"Well, look who decided to pull themselves away from their mate and join the grown-up world," she teased.

"Like you weren't worse when you got mated. If I remember correctly, you didn't show up for a couple of weeks."

Brownyn smirked. "Yes, my sweet baby knows how to sweep me off my feet," she gushed.

Bronwyn and Maria had been mated for about three years, and it was love at first sight, and they would do anything for each other. Frost wanted the same for him and Zane.

"Hey, did you see Bluebell and his mate?"

"Mate!"

Frost hadn't seen his blue-haired cousin the entire time they were in Wynter Spell. The main reason was he was too wrapped up in Zane to notice anyone else. But he was surprised to hear his cousin had a mate. He knew how dedicated Bluebell was to his job.

"Yes, word through the grapevine was something big was happening with Bluebell, his mate, and his mate's kids."

Frost's head was filled with questions, like who Bluebell's mate was and where the hell the kids came from. He made a mental note that once he got some time, he would really pay a visit to Bluebell.

"How did you hear all of this?"

"Thomas."

Thomas was another of their cousins, a jin searching for a mate. But said mate would have to find Thomas's magical lamp first. When Frost had told Zane that his family was complicated, he wasn't kidding. After gossiping with

Brownyn about everything he'd missed out on while they'd been home, he went to work.

Around half-past three, Frost started putting away his work. His brows furrowed when he realized he hadn't heard from Zane all day. Grabbing his cellphone, he called Zane but ended up hanging up when the phone rang until the voicemail picked up. Setting his phone down, Frost tapped his fingers on his desk.

Something was wrong. He didn't know why he thought that, Frost just knew. Zane would never let his call go more than two rings and would call him back immediately if he missed his call. He quickly sent off a text and waited for a breath before picking his phone back up and calling again; when it went unanswered once more, Frost shot up from his desk and ran to Brownyn.

"I'm leaving. Something is wrong with Zane."

"What do you mean?"

"I don't know, but I'm not wasting any more time." Before she could say any more, he disappeared.

CHAPTER FIFTEEN

Zane groaned, opening his eyes. He had a splitting head from the pits of hell, and he didn't know where the hell it came from. The last thing he remembered was after putting Hannah in bed so she could take a nap, he had opened the door and saw Megan on the other side, before his world tilted back.

Megan! Hannah!

Zane went to stand but noticed he was handcuffed at the wrist, and his leg was on fire, and it was spreading throughout his body.

Fuck, silver handcuffs. What the fuck is going on? Zane looked around, recognizing Megan's basement since he'd helped move a thing or two over the years of their friendship. *What the fuck am I doing in Megan's basement?*

Zane did not want to think about what it meant. Why would Megan do this to him, and how did she know to use silver to weaken him when he'd never told her he was a werewolf? And more importantly, where was Hannah? He didn't think Megan would hurt her, but he couldn't take the chance. The door opened, and footsteps came down the stairs. Zane looked up when he saw Megan coming down the stairs.

"Oh, you're awake," Megan said, moving over to him and jumping into his lap, resting her head on his chest and running her hand through his hair. Zane's stomach turned, ready to revolt, but he held it in. "Zane, this feels so nice. I'm so happy."

"Where's Hannah?"

"She's upstairs eating dinner." Megan leaned back, cupping Zane's cheek and gazing into his face. "I finally have you all to myself." She rested her head back on his chest. "We're going to be happy, Zane. Me, you, and Hannah, like it should have been."

Sweat beaded on his forehead, and the headache grew more intense. Zane closed his eyes and bit his tongue, filling his mouth with blood, and he could taste the poison from the silver taking effect. If he didn't get released soon he would die.

"How did you get me down here?" he asked, hoping to distract her.

"It wasn't easy," she told him. "But I've been practicing." She raised her head. "Do you know how long I've dreamed of doing this with you?"

Zane shook his head.

"Years, let me tell you. From the first time Arizona introduced you to her family."

Zane's eyes widened, but he quickly masked his shock, hoping she'd say more.

"I know you don't remember me. After all, we've been friends for this long and you still don't know that Arizona and I were related. Distantly, of course, but still blood-related, nonetheless. Perfect princess Arizona, born without powers but adored by everyone." She began breathing heavily, hopping off Zane's lap. "But little old me, born with the same ailment, was cast aside. Everyone thinks our coven is accepting, so why was I seen as a mistake?"

Zane was shocked to hear that one, Megan was a witch, and two, that she was related to Arizona. *So she knew I was a werewolf,* Zane reasoned. *All this time she knew what I was and never said anything. Why?*

"Do you know how many times I wished I had her life? People who loved her and never cared if she had powers or not. But my parents did. They compared me to her. Why can't you be more like Arizona, they would say. She might not have powers, but at least she still practices her spells. Fuck, they were annoying."

"So what does this have to do with me?" Zane asked through clenched teeth. He was worried about Hannah, contrary to Megan's words assuring him she was fine. "Are you mad because I forgot who you were?"

"At first, I was mad you didn't know who I was. It's why I let you continue to think I was just a simple-minded human who knew nothing about shifters, but I got over it and figured once we became a couple, I would tell you everything." Megan leaned in and kissed Zane on his lips gently. "Wanting her life meant I could have you," she said softly as a glazed look crossed her eyes. "Why should she be happy with a handsome, strong, alpha werewolf when I had nothing? I followed her to Italy."

Zane gasped at hearing that but didn't say anything.

"I planned on killing her, but luck was on my side, and someone else did the job for me instead. Do you know how much I rejoiced in her death? That's how much I hated the perfect princess. But it broke my heart seeing you so sad at her loss. After I moved here, I was glad you didn't recognize me after all. We'd only met once, and your eyes were on

Arizona the entire time. After she died, I bided my time. I befriended you and helped you with Hannah. I tried to fill the gap of being a mother to her, hoping that one day you would see what a good mate I could be for you."

Her voice began to rise the more she spoke as her anger took over. Zane, on the other hand, was not doing so well. The poison was taking effect, and his body was shaking.

"Why, Zane?" She grabbed him by the shoulders. "I love you so much and yet you went out and found another mate after you swore you'd never take on another. So, why him? What does that fucking fae have that I don't? After all that I did, you should have been mine. I would have killed for you, yet you ignored me. I cherished that bitch's daughter as if she were mine, and you never once told me you liked me. Or even invited me over for fucking Christmas dinner. But with him after just a few weeks together you travel to meet his family when I'm right next door."

Zane raised a brow. "How do you know about that?"

"Hannah told me. For as long as we've known each other, Zane, I thought you were warming up to me. Fuck, I would have settled for just being your bed partner, but you turned around and found someone else when I was right here." She paused, panting as her face moved closer to his to press their lips together.

"It was you that night, wasn't it?" Zane asked, finally speaking. "You were the one that broke into my house."

"Yes, but who knew you'd have some freak dressed like an elf watching our sweet Hannah."

"Look who's calling someone a freak," Zane mumbled.

"I wasn't going to hurt Hannah, Zane. I just missed her and wanted to see her. Despite being a product of Arizona, she is half yours, and I love her. Being a mom to her is just as important as being your lover. But now I don't have to worry about that. After tonight, you will be mine. And we'll all be together, far away from this place, and not even a fae will be able to find you."

Zane opened his mouth to ask what she meant by that but was stopped by his cellphone ringing. Zane knew who was calling, he recognized the ringtone. It was Frost. Zane knew if he didn't answer, his mate would pick up that something was wrong. Neither he nor Megan moved or breathed. They stared at each other as if they wanted the phone to stop ringing. Seconds later, his phone alerted him that he had a text. Still, neither he nor Megan made a move. However, when his phone rang again, Megan rushed for his pocket, and, with every ounce of his strength, he rocked the chair with her holding on to him and was happy when it toppled over.

The chair broke with the force, putting Zane at an advantage where he could move but was too weak because he was still wearing the silver handcuffs, poisoning his blood, and Megan was still trying to get to his phone.

"Give me that damn phone," she growled.

They tossed and turned, with Zane pushing her away, but she was fast attacking him again until he kicked her away from him, causing her to hit her back against a shelf and knocking her out. He waited for the guilt since it was the first time in his life he'd ever done anything so harsh to a woman. Zane pulled at the handcuffs, but all he was doing was bruising his wrist, which was bleeding from the earlier chair fall, pushing more of the poison into his body even faster.

"Zane, where are you!"

He looked up when he heard Frost calling his name. He

struggled to his feet, gasping for breath as he took one step, only to fall to his knees. His body shook from the poison.

I need to get these damn handcuffs off. I have to get out of here.

He turned his head to the side when Megan groaned, waking up. Moving as quickly as he could, he reached her side and was about to search for the key when she raised her leg and kicked him in the stomach before he could stop her. Zane doubled over in pain because he was so damn weak.

"Look what you made me do," she screamed in his face. "All I wanted was for us to have a happy ending. But you had to ruin it."

"You're fucking crazy," Zane said between gasps as bile filled his mouth. His body ached, and it felt like he was about to die, but he had to hold on because he knew Frost would save him.

Megan grabbed him by the shirt and slapped him across the face. "Who the fuck do you think you're talking to. Don't you see that I have the upper hand? A frail, magicless woman like myself has power over a big, strong alpha like you." She trailed a hand down to the handcuff. "But I guess I have these to thank, or you'd already have kicked my ass. I know how strong you are, Zane. I just need you weak enough to get you away from here."

Zane let her talk as he saw Bronwyn quietly coming down the stairs out of the corner of his eyes. He turned his attention back to Megan, seeing so much anger in her eyes. He honestly never thought of her as anything but a friend. But maybe in the back of his mind, he'd known she had feelings for him, and he ignored them, hoping she'd move on. Perhaps he'd used her feelings regarding Hannah, which he had to own up to.

"I'm sorry, Megan," he said to her and watched her eyes soften.

"What? Why are you apologizing to me now?"

"For this?" Brownyn grabbed her by the shoulder, turned her around, and punched her in the face. Megan released Zane, who fell to the floor weakly as she staggered back but didn't fall.

"Who the hell are you?" Megan growled.

"Someone you should be very afraid of, bitch," Brownyn said, raising her hand and slapping Megan across her face.

"Zane," Frost shouted, his mate coming over to hug him. "I'm so glad you're all right."

"Silver, Hannah," he panted, looking away from Brownyn, who was beating the hell out of Megan, as Frost leaned back and grabbed the cuffs on his wrists.

"Hannah is fine. She's with Nyx. You don't have to worry. She has no clue what's happening here. We need to get these off of you. I'm so glad Hannah never took those earrings off. That's how I was able to find you both."

Zane closed his eyes in relief. "Good." He could feel his body growing weaker by the second. He didn't know how long he had been out or how long he had been wearing the handcuffs, but he gathered it was enough time to bring him to this weakened state. Zane opened his eyes and looked down when he felt one of the handcuffs fall off his wrists. He glanced around and noticed Megan tied up in a corner and Brownyn shaking her hand.

"Fuck, she had a tough-ass jaw." She walked over to them. "Here, I got the key for you, and you already found metal shears."

"We need to get him out of here and get him some

help," Frost said. Zane closed his eyes again as his head fell on Frost's shoulder.

"I called Maria. She's on her way."

"Thank you, Brownyn," he heard Frost say.

Zane wanted to speak or move, now that the handcuffs were off, but he was still too weak to even lift his hand to cup Frost's face.

"I love you," he said to Frost mentally.

Frost kissed his forehead. "I love you too."

That was the last thing that Zane heard before passing out.

EPILOGUE

New Year's ball

Zane leaned against the bar, sipping his gin and tonic, waiting for his special guest to arrive. He couldn't believe the fuckery that had happened a few days ago. Megan had somehow had him handcuffed in her basement. Zane still couldn't recall what had happened after he had opened the door or how he had ended up at her house.

He didn't think he would ever find out since Megan wasn't saying anything. Instead of calling the cops, Frost called the supernatural council to handle things since it involved a witch and a werewolf. Suffice to say, Megan would never again see the light of day.

According to Frost, he and Brownyn found their house in disarray. After checking the entire place, he tracked Hannah using the jewelry he made her. When he found Hannah, she was eating. Frost had called Nyx without alerting Hannah that anything was wrong. Once Nyx took Hannah away, Frost went in search of Zane, and that was when Brownyn found them in the basement.

Maria, Bownyn's mate, was a doctor and a witch, so she

took over and healed Zane, cleansing his blood of the poison. He had been out for twenty-four hours, and during that time, Nyx had kept Hannah away from the house. Frost did not want the little girl to worry about losing another parent. After waking up, Zane spent much time with Hannah, who weirdly hadn't asked about Megan.

Maybe one day, when she's much older, I'll tell her what happened.

Zane looked at his watch, noticing it was five minutes to midnight, and wondered where Frost was since he hadn't seen his mate all day. Brownyn had done an excellent job putting the party all together, and the Eclipse looked like something out of a fairy tale. Each room had a different theme, and his employees and special guests were having a ball with the scavenger hunt. He liked the luxurious home, and they would move in after the ball. He and Frost had a long talk, and after the whole Megan thing, they decided it was time for a change of residence.

"Mister Blood-Moon, this is a wonderful party," Cherry Blackstone told him as she got a drink from the bar. She was dressed as a princess, like most of the women were at the ball.

Zane had been dressed as Prince Charming. It was an easy outfit to pull together by simply wearing a tuxedo and bow tie. He had no clue what Frost would be wearing. He looked at his watch again and saw that a couple of minutes had passed since he was lost in thought. He was about to pull out his cellphone and call Frost when Carlton, one of his employees, gasped. Zane looked at him and followed his eyeline, and his breath caught in his chest.

On the stairs landing stood the most handsome fae he had ever seen. Moderately long snow-white hair braided on the right side, pointed ears, and black tattoo markings that started from his hairline disappeared into the high collar of his light blue jacket that flared out in the back like a bridal train. Zane could tell the markings were not accurate because Frost's were usually a lighter, brighter color that seemed to glow. Frost wore a white harness with transparent crystal-like wings sprouting from his back.

Zane heard whispering around him, but he ignored it, and without thought, started walking toward the stairs, taking them two at a time. In less than a few seconds, he was standing in front of Frost where he noticed the crown nestled in his hair.

"It's almost midnight," Zane said, wrapping his arms around Frost.

"Then I came just in time." He circled Zane's neck and pressed their lips together. Distantly in the background, Zane heard the countdown to midnight, but he couldn't care less. The person with whom he was going to have his new beginning and many others was in his arms.

THANK YOU

Dear Readers,

Thank you, for taking to the time to support me, and I hope you enjoy reading Frost which is an extension of His Magical Touch and some of the Pryde Shifter Series. I loved stepping into this world and writing new characters. I hope that you will continue to read and share this book.

With all of my thanks and appreciation

Giovanna (Gia) Reaves

ABOUT THE AUTHOR

Giovanna (Gia) Reaves is my alter ego, who is a dreamer. I spend my days and nights dreaming and thinking of the worlds I want to create with words. I started writing about three years ago, when I was introduced to the world of fan fiction.

I loved the idea of creating a new world around characters that people already knew about. And ones that are original of my own making. I have written two novels and a few free stories.

I am a mother, wife, and a military veteran. I enjoy trying new things such as traveling, cooking, and reading. I try to incorporate some of the things I have experienced into my books.

Currently living in Newport, RI with my two favorite men. If I am not hidden in my cave writing, I love to read and spend time with my hubby and son. I love listening to R and B along with neo soul when I am writing.

When I'm not writing, I am trying to perfect my baking and decorating skills or try to pick up something new. I love spending time with my husband and son playing video games and traveling.

Want to know more about me follow me on Social Media or send me an email.

GotRomance@giareaves.com

Sign up for my Ream https://reamstories.com/giovanna reaves

BOOKS BY GIOVANNA REAVES

Goliath's Mate: G-Force Federation (Book Three)

Check out the Vale Valley Series

Season One: A Vale Valley Winter Romance

Season Two: A Vale Valley Valentine Romance

Season Three: A Vale Valley Summer Romance

Audiobooks

Jordan's Pryde

The Cowboy's Baby

HIS MAGICAL TOUCH

With one wish and a little luck, he has the perfect touch.

Luca Rossi is a practical man in thoughts and actions. He's always counted himself extremely fortunate but never would've believed there's real magic behind it. As a divorced father, his priority is protecting and providing for his three children. And after his nanny quit, Luca desperately searches for a new one. Luca finds it hard to trust the care of his children to anyone until a blue-haired, blue-eyed man shows up on his doorstep and changes how he sees the world.

Bluebell Boroson is an elf-witch and a wish agent who works for Santa's Workshop. He gets great enjoyment from granting the desires in others' hearts. After failing his last assignment and being put on desk duty, Bluebell is plagued by self-doubt. When he is given a second chance, Bluebell isn't sure if he is up to the job. One, he has to pretend to be a nanny, and two, there's a deadline to fulfill this wish request. Bluebell cannot fail, or he will have to give up a job he loves.

When Luca and Bluebell meet, neither can deny their underlying attraction toward each other. But between misunderstandings and facing their own challenges, they never imagined that they could change each other's lives with one wish and a bit of luck.

For fans of the bestselling multi-author Vale Valley *and* Valleywood *series,* His Magical Touch *is a standalone novel in the same universe but not a part of either series, but expect a couple of familiar faces to drop by. This is a feel-good story with little angst, mpreg, insta-attraction/lust/love, and a lot of magic.*

Get it Now - https://www.giareaves.com/giaebooks/p/hismagicaltouch

ANUBIS'S STAR

Doubt has never been part of Anubis's vocabulary - he's confident, driven, and knows exactly what he desires, even if it means he's given up finding his forever one. Yet, upon seeing Star, everything changes - from their immediate attraction and desire to his mysterious background. Despite his misgivings, fate keeps pushing them closer, and neither Anubis nor Star can deny their affection for one another.

Thrust into the world of magic, young up-and-coming actor Star Rueng is hesitant to get entangled in love again. After being hurt by trusting the wrong man with his heart and career, he decides he doesn't need the heartache. But the moment he sets eyes on Anubis Ahket, he is enthralled to the point of obsession. As Star struggles to comprehend his newfound world, he soon realizes he cannot help but fall for a man he believes is too good for him.

With only a spark of attraction, the fates never get it wrong.

Read Anubis's Star

VALLEYWOOD SEASON TWO SERIES

Nestled on the shores of Lake Erie, Pennsylvania, there is a major city that no one has ever heard of. Valleywood is home to some of the country's wealthiest and most powerful magical beings. It's a commerce, entertainment, and finance hub in the supernatural world. Unlike the quaint and picturesque Vale Valley to the south, Valleywood is a loud and vibrant city--and they have the seedy underbelly to go with it.

Stripped of his powers by his father, Mayor Loki

Boroson oversees the city. And what interests Loki usually means mischief and drama. But over the years, the magic of this city has faded, and along with that comes the threat that this cornerstone of life for so many people might one day vanish for good.

In an age where gods live among men, love might be the only magic that matters.

Get the entire second season